Best Laid Plans

Elizabeth Palmer

CRIMSON
ROMANCE
Avon, Massachusetts

This edition published by
Crimson Romance
an imprint of F+W Media, Inc.
10151 Carver Road, Suite 200
Blue Ash, Ohio 45242

www.crimsonromance.com

Copyright © 2012 by Elizabeth Palmer

ISBN 10: 1-4405-5099-9
ISBN 13: 978-1-4405-5099-7
eISBN 10: 1-4405-5098-0
eISBN 13: 978-1-4405-5098-0

This is a work of fiction.

Names, characters, corporations, institutions, organizations, events, or locales in this novel are either the product of the author's imagination or, if real, used fictitiously. The resemblance of any character to actual persons (living or dead) is entirely coincidental.

Chapter One

Violet Gallagher felt like she was all alone at her own going-away party, even though a hundred people smiled and applauded as they waited for her to speak. After wiping away her sudden tears with a manicured fingertip, she turned on her brightest evening-news smile and took a deep breath.

"Please excuse me," she said, once the room was quiet. "It just sank in that I'm leaving Wickham and all the wonderful friends I've made here."

As Richard Rayburn, her co-anchor at WWIC, had said when he introduced her, she was moving up to the station's network affiliate in Boston. The promotion was the achievement of a decade-long goal, yet she felt no joy in her accomplishment this evening. Wickham, a close-knit seaside community about sixty miles from Boston, had been warm and welcoming, and she would miss it — but she didn't think that was the problem.

Just in case, she turned to her producer, seated next to the dais at the head table. "If they don't like me in Boston, can I come back?"

The hoots and whistles that followed gave her the opportunity to scan the faces in the ballroom. Her coworkers from WWIC were all there, of course, and members of the community ranging from her downstairs neighbor to the mayor. A man she didn't recognize caught her eye and winked, and she smiled back. Could she have met such a gorgeous man and forgotten? Matt Macintyre, a local builder and president of the Chamber of Commerce, sat next to the handsome stranger. He grinned and gave her a thumbs-up signal.

Conspicuously absent, however, was the face of anyone she could consider more than just a *friend*. Her mother and stepfather were on a cruise they had planned long before her promotion was announced, and her twin brother Seth was trying an important case at home in California and couldn't get away.

When she had imagined this proud moment — and she had, many times — there was always a special someone in the crowd clapping harder than everyone else, the one person whose approval mattered. But the calculated planning that had been so effective for reaching her career goals had gotten her nowhere when it came to love. Now she vowed that once she was settled in Boston, she'd make a new plan. A *love* plan.

"There's really only one thing I want to say. Thank you, everyone, for making the last five years the best of my life."

As she stepped away from the podium after her short speech, she was surrounded by guests who wanted to give her an air-kiss or clasp her hand and tell her how much she'd be missed. Within fifteen minutes, however, the group had dispersed and she was left standing alone. The last time she'd felt as awkward had been at her eighth-grade dinner dance, when she'd been certain everyone except her was part of a couple.

She snatched a glass of champagne off the tray of a passing waiter and drained it in three gulps while considering the advice her brother had given her when he'd called just before the party.

"Be yourself," he'd told her, only to immediately amend his statement. "Except more spontaneous. Don't be afraid to leave some things to chance."

Resolving to be more outgoing, and, yes, more spontaneous, she headed for the dessert table, where Matt caught her in a bear hug.

"Oh, Violet, I wanted to ask you out the first time I met you, but I was too shy." His booming voice caught the attention of everyone around them; people who knew him, which included almost everyone, laughed and shook their heads. Shy, he was not. "Now it's too late."

"If I'd ever seen you in a tuxedo, I wouldn't have waited for you to do the asking." Although she knew he was joking, his flirting always made her feel feminine and desirable. He was at least a decade older than Violet, but if he'd ever asked her for a date, she'd have said yes in a flash.

"Have you met my nephew, Jake Macintyre?" He turned to the side and revealed a tall, broad-shouldered man with golden hair that curled over his forehead and around his ears — the mystery man who had winked at her during her speech.

Although he resembled his uncle in height and coloring, Jake was slimmer, and his features were more classically handsome — less hunky construction worker and more romantic-comedy leading-man. His boyish appearance, and the fact that he was Matt's nephew, fooled her at first into thinking he must be visiting from college. Then he smiled, and the crinkles around his dark amber eyes said he must be close to her age, in his early to mid-thirties.

"I don't make a habit of crashing going-away parties." He held her hand long enough for her to notice how it engulfed hers. His skin was warm and dry.

"But he often crashes other kinds!" Matt's laughter brought her back to earth, and she withdrew her hand from Jake's and switched her empty flute of champagne for a full one. Her hand trembled as she downed a mouthful of the cool, bubbly drink.

"Jake's visiting from Boston," Matt continued, "and I didn't feel right leaving him home alone."

"Really? He seems like a big boy to me." Her face felt so hot she had to resist the urge to fan herself. *Spontaneous*, she reminded herself, not foolish.

Both men laughed. "Family story," Jake said. "I couldn't be left alone or I'd escape."

Even three glasses of champagne weren't enough to make her ask him what *that* meant. He didn't seem like a dangerous escapee from a mental institution, but, being a veteran newswoman, she knew those people never did.

WWIC's anchorman lurched toward them and clapped Jake

on the shoulder. "You're Jake Macintyre. I have a call in to your agent about doing a story on your book. I'm Richard Rayburn."

The two men shook hands, although Jake appeared annoyed by the interruption. His gaze flicked back to Violet even as he spoke to Richard. "I'm at your disposal, although you'll have to wait."

"Lucky Richard." Had she said that out loud? Judging from the way all three men were staring at her, she had.

Nothing to do but tip up her glass and take another big hit. She'd been out of the loop at work because of her move, and wasn't familiar with Jake's work. She would ask him about it if the opportunity arose, but experience told her if she waited, he'd volunteer the information. People loved to talk about their work.

"Do you know Violet?" Richard asked Jake. "She's my former co-anchor and fusure wife. I mean, my *fusure* wife."

Violet's burst of laughter sent bubbles up her nose. She'd never heard Richard mispronounce a word before, and he'd just done it twice.

"You may laugh, but I know you're secretly in love with me. There's also a slight chance you've had too much to drink. Or I have." Richard wore the spurned-puppy face that always tugged at her heart.

He'd told her he was considering a move to Boston himself, and said he hoped to take their relationship to a "new level" once they were no longer coworkers. On paper, he seemed like perfect husband and father material, but she'd always thought of him as "just Richard," her work partner and now her friend.

"I do love you." At that moment she loved everyone. "And I haven't had too much to drink, I'm just being spontaneous!"

"Hold this for the lady," Jake said to Richard, reaching for her glass. "You can have it back after you dance with me."

She took a final gulp and handed the empty flute to Richard, then allowed Jake to press his hand against the small of her back and propel her onto the dance floor. The silk of her designer black-and-ivory slip-dress was so sheer he might have been touching her naked skin, and the heat of his hand through it made her shiver. When he turned to face her and took her right hand in his left, tightening his hold on her back, he was grinning.

"Are you enjoying yourself?" Even in three-inch heels, she had to tip her head uncomfortably far back to see his face. The view, however, was worth it.

His smile widened, displaying perfect teeth. He was better-looking than any anchorman she knew. Even Richard, renowned for his chiseled features and thick head of hair, seemed a bit foppish in comparison.

"I was just thinking how much I like your dress."

Then he drew her close and began to dance with an ease she'd only seen in men of her stepfather's generation. David Gallagher had taught her to dance in the days before that eighth grade event — unnecessarily, as it turned out, since no one asked her — and made her feel like a princess despite her awkward stumbling. But when he'd turned to her mother, his queen, and whirled her around the kitchen, Violet had watched and known she was in the presence of great love. Her long-suffering mother, and she and Seth too, had been rescued by the kind, steady gentleman. That night she'd written on her first list of goals, "marry a man like David."

Something about Jake reminded her of her stepfather, something more than his skill at the foxtrot. But his approximate age, that he lived in Boston, and that he was a writer, were all she knew about him. Oh, and one more thing. He was knee-weakening, heart-hammering gorgeous. A handsome author might make the perfect partner off the dance floor as well.

Maybe it was time to get started on the new plan.

"I'm glad I crashed your party." As he spoke he pulled her closer, and she both heard his words and felt them as a breath of warm air against her ear.

The tantalizing gap between them disappeared, and once again she was conscious of the flimsiness of her dress. She felt the hard muscles of his chest and his thighs as he led her in the dance, first advancing, then retreating. Never had a first dance with a man been so effortless; she moved with Jake as easily as she breathed.

To her delight, he didn't relinquish his hold on her when the music stopped. "We'll wait for the next one." His grin was gone, but his intense gaze held her in place.

Unable to speak, she only nodded.

When the bandleader announced they were having technical difficulties and needed to take a short break, Jake groaned, then threw back his head and laughed. "I guess this means I'll have to let you go. But do me a favor, and back away slowly. The last time dancing had this effect on me, I was in high school."

She stepped away, but didn't let go of his hand. "Come with me." The door to the terrace was just a few feet away, and they slipped out into the relative coolness of the June night. Chinese lanterns provided soft illumination, and a half-crescent moon hung in the sky above them. She walked to the white iron railing and gazed up at the stars.

"This is so much better than my eighth-grade dinner dance."

He laughed, then placed his hand over hers on the railing. "It's hard to believe beautiful Violet Gallagher was ever a wallflower, but I suppose anything's possible."

"I hate to say this — I *really* hate to say this — but I was a late bloomer."

The laugh she was expecting didn't come. "A bloom worth waiting for," he said.

Then Violet *did* laugh. "Is that the best you've got?"

A furrow appeared on his forehead. "Did that sound like a line? You'll have to forgive me, I'm out of practice. In fact, I've never been any good at this."

Coming from a broad-shouldered, six-foot-tall man with altar-boy curls, his disclaimer sounded even more like a line. Unless he really had been locked up somewhere? And what exactly was the "this" he'd never been good at?

"Umm, Jake, I don't know very much about you . . ."

"No, but I know a lot about *you*." He took a step closer, and she turned her body away from the railing so they were face-to-face. His eyes were so intensely focused on hers, she felt like he could see inside her.

"You've just seen me do the news. You don't really *know* me." It was amazing how many people thought they did, but she didn't expect that from this man.

He shook his head, like a teacher who was disappointed with his student's answer. "No, it isn't that. It's your eyes, those incredible blue eyes. I see a passion for life in them, and I know you're someone who puts your whole heart into everything you do."

She closed her eyes then, afraid he would see she'd put her whole heart into her work for ten years, and was now feeling empty and alone on what should have been a night of celebration. His lips touched hers, so gently at first she had to reopen her eyes to see if it was happening. Then she closed them again and yielded to his kiss, wondering if Jake might be the man who could fill that emptiness.

"Listen," she said, when the kiss ended and she caught her breath, "I have to go inside and mingle. But if you'd like to give me a ride home later . . ."

Violet didn't go home with men she'd just met. But his uncle was a pillar of the community, and she'd promised Seth she'd be more spontaneous. Promise or no promise, she wanted to be with this man tonight. Without even the thinnest layer of silk between them.

He seemed surprised, and delighted. "Are you sure that's what you want?"

His hesitation touched her. Instead of answering she kissed him, rising up on tiptoe and breathing in his masculine sunshine-and-sweat scent. The second kiss, which sent an electric shock through the center of her body, was both a promise and a dare.

Violet reeled when Jake released her, struggling to stay on her feet. She wondered just how long she'd have to make small talk before it would be polite for her to leave her own party. As she walked back through the door to the ballroom with him behind her, she felt his fingers caress the base of her spine, and then slip lower. When he squeezed the rounded flesh there, she decided she didn't give a hoot about good manners.

*

Jake hovered on the periphery of the ballroom and watched as Violet laughed and chatted with a group of her friends. How soon could he expect her to give him the signal she was ready to leave? He decided to move to the bar. A strong drink in his hand might keep it from shaking.

"Give me the best single-malt Scotch you have."

"Put it on my tab, John."

Jake, recognizing Richard-the-anchorman's unaccented speech from the nightly news he watched whenever he visited Matt, turned to him with a smile.

"Thanks. I'll return the favor someday."

Richard took a swallow of his drink and turned his head in Violet's direction. It wasn't lost on Jake that he knew exactly where to find her.

"It's like that, is it?" Considering what had just transpired out on the balcony, Jake doubted very much the two were a couple, but the other man's desire was written all over him.

Richard shook his head, his expression mournful. "I've tried, but she won't date a coworker. I haven't told her yet, but I had an interview with a cable channel in Boston yesterday. I've always wanted to be a producer, and if I'm nearby but not working with her, I'm sure I'll have a chance. We're perfect together."

As the two men watched, Violet moved on to another group of well-wishers. She tugged at a strand of her glossy black hair that had escaped from her up-do, and Jake envisioned himself pulling out the pins and letting it fall over her creamy skin. As he imagined the feel of it against his own skin, he gulped down a mouthful of the Scotch and choked.

Richard clapped him on the back, much harder than necessary. "Is this a good idea, old man?" He cut his eyes toward Violet, so there was no doubt what he meant.

He blurted out the truth. "No."

When his uncle asked him if he wanted to tag along to the party and meet his "dream girl," he couldn't resist. They'd often joked about the fact that Jake *had* to watch the WWIC news whenever he was in Wickham; Matt would tell him to put his tongue back in his mouth. There was something so sweet and innocent, and yet at the same time so sexy, about her. Would the reality of Violet in the flesh be a disappointment?

In any case, there had been no thought — certainly no *intention* — of anything beyond a few hours of flirtation. But Violet had *not* been a disappointment, and she had invited him to extend the evening. Jake never said no to delightful and unexpected opportunities, or to women as attractive as Violet.

Richard misunderstood Jake's negative reply. He nodded, satisfied. "Good. The last thing she needs is someone like you messing up her life."

Violet had moved closer to the bar, and Jake heard her tell someone she needed to make a phone call. It was the moment he'd been anticipating ever since they returned from the balcony — the signal.

He downed the rest of his drink and thumped the unlucky anchorman on the back. "Thanks for the drink, Rayburn, but I have to run." Since he didn't plan to take it, he didn't thank him for his advice.

*

Best Laid Plans

Unlocking the door to her apartment thirty minutes later, Violet felt a moment of uncertainty. Did this need to happen tonight? Jake lived in Boston; they would be able to see each other after she moved. Maybe she would even be sober. But then he leaned up against her back and kissed the exposed nape of her neck, and she thought she would melt into a puddle on the floor. When she turned to him with the key still in the lock so she could feel his length against the front of her, he pushed his tongue into her mouth again and her doubts disappeared.

"Inside . . . " she gasped.

After turning on a light in the entryway, she led the way around the stacks of boxes to the bedroom where she'd slept alone for more than two years, ever since the breakup of her last, brief relationship. Once she reached the bed she turned to him, wanting to leave the next move up to him.

"You're lovely." She could feel his hand tremble as he slid the zipper down at the back of her dress. It dropped to the floor in one fluid motion, leaving her naked except for lacy black panties and her shoes.

As he had earlier on the dance floor, he put his arm around her back and pulled her to him. This time there was no polite space between them. He was still fully dressed, and the roughness of his clothing against her naked skin was incredibly exciting. Even so, she reached up and undid the black bow tie, sliding her other hand inside his jacket at the same time and slipping it off his shoulder.

He joined in her efforts to remove his clothes, beginning with undoing his belt, but it was a slow process because of frequent stops to slide his hands over her breasts and bottom. Her nipples were stiff from the touch of his fingers, and she was more ready than she'd ever been. Had been ready, in fact, ever since that second kiss on the terrace. She couldn't wait for him to discover the effect he'd had on her.

Before he was fully naked himself, he yanked her panties down below her knees and guided her backward until she was sitting on the edge of the bed. Kneeling in front of her, he slid them down as far as her ankles, removed both her shoes, and pulled the scrap of black lace over her feet.

"This is no longer a formal affair, and I'm feeling overdressed." He stood and began to unbutton his shirt with what she considered agonizing slowness. When he sat on the edge of the bed with his back to her to remove his shoes and socks, she leaned over and caressed the back of his neck. As soon as his hands were free, she grasped the collar of his shirt and slid it down and off his arms, revealing a tanned, well-muscled back with a patch of whiter, ridged and puckered skin covering most of his right shoulder blade. It appeared to be a scar from a bad burn, but she knew this wasn't the time or place to ask him about it.

He stood again and stripped off his remaining clothes, then turned and faced her. She was pleased to see he looked as good without the tuxedo as he'd looked in it. Finally he grinned and bent over her, tantalizing her with a probing kiss while maintaining a strangers-on-the-dance-floor distance between their naked bodies.

"Are you trying to make me beg?" she managed to gasp when the kiss ended.

His own breathing was ragged. "I didn't expect this to happen, and I'm not exactly. . . prepared."

"Prepared?" She felt like her head was full of champagne bubbles. What was he talking about?

"Do you have protection?"

"Oh!" She dragged herself to the head of the bed and slid open the drawer to her nightstand. Shoved way in the back, there was a strip of condoms.

"Thank God," he said, accepting them like a prize and ripping one open. "Otherwise I might have been tempted to do something foolish."

Tell me about it. Then she — either spontaneously or foolishly, she wasn't sure which — opened her arms, her legs, and her heart to a man she'd just met.

*

Violet woke up with a mouth full of cotton in a head that felt like it belonged to someone else. She sat up gingerly and reached for the glass of tepid water on her nightstand, knocking Jake's watch to the floor in the process. *Jake.* She smiled through her pain at the memory of last night. The first time they'd made love had been frantic and fast, but the second — and the third — had surpassed any expectation of sexual bliss she'd ever had, as orgasm after orgasm rippled through her.

She heard the water running and realized Jake was in the shower. Would it, she wondered, be too forward of her to join him? The thought made her smile. After last night, nothing seemed off limits. But the shower came to a stop before she could act on her impulse.

After retrieving the watch and gulping down the glass of water, she slipped out of bed and pulled on the robe she'd left draped over her bedroom chair. She removed one or two hairpins still clinging to her disheveled hair, and brushed it out in front of the bureau.

"In that kimono, with your dark hair down, you look like a princess. It's a good thing I didn't walk in before you belted the sash." He'd come out of the bathroom with his curly hair still damp from the shower, and was rolling up the sleeves on last night's white dress shirt.

"That's a good thing?" She opened her arms to him, but his embrace lasted only seconds. Sighing, he kissed her forehead and let her go.

She handed him the watch, which he slid onto his wrist. Had she misunderstood something last night? It had been the beginning of something special, she was sure of it. Now he was acting like he couldn't wait to leave. Her heart lurched in her chest. What if he was *married*? Why hadn't she asked more questions?

"I have to get back to my brother's place in Boston. My flight isn't until midnight, but I still have packing to do."

Had he said something to her about a trip? Maybe he was going away on a book promotion. Or was he in a hurry to get out of there because last night hadn't meant anything to him?

"Jake, I just want to say I don't sleep with men I've just met . . ."

He put his arms around her, and this time he held on. "I know. But of course we only had the one night, and we had to grab the opportunity. It's making this difficult, though. I've never minded before."

"Minded what?"

"Leaving the States. I feel like a soldier, going off to war and leaving the world's prettiest girl at home."

She pulled away. Barefoot, it was even more difficult to meet his eyes. "Jake, where exactly are you going?"

"Russia for six months, then straight to Tibet for six more." He frowned. "But you knew that, right? Richard knew what I do and I thought you did too . . ."

She rubbed her aching temples and sank down onto the rumpled bed. "I'm sorry, I probably should know what you wrote, but I've been preoccupied with the job change."

He got down on his knees in front of her. "Violet, I'm the one who should be sorry. I feel like I've taken advantage of you. I'm not really a writer, I'm a photojournalist. The book I just finished is called *An American in South Africa*. I immerse myself in the day-to-day life of a place for six months or a year, and then I work with my editor for a few months, choosing the pictures and writing the text. It's what I've been doing in Boston this spring."

"Oh." This is what comes of being spontaneous, she told herself. You find the man you think could be Mr. Right, have the best sex of your life, and then find out he's a globe-trotting adventurer. Worse than her father, who had been constantly on the road with his band while she was growing up, eventually resulting in the break-up of her parents' marriage. She had pictured an author as someone who was always home, pounding the keyboard in his office down the hall. This was worse, even, than if he'd been married.

"'Oh'? That's all you have to say?"

Jake's distress was genuine, she knew. He believed she'd been fully aware last night was going to be a one-night stand, or at best a same-time-next-year scenario.

"Listen, there's been no harm done here." She forced herself to smile. "Last night was great. Not my usual style, I admit, but fun. Nobody needs to be sorry." She didn't tell him it had seemed like so much more than *fun* to her at the time.

He stood up, checking his watch, and she rose with him.

"No time for coffee?"

She was relieved when he shook his head. No sense prolonging this goodbye; she had a life to get on with.

"Can I look you up in Boston when I get back?" he asked at the door.

"Of course!" She accepted his light kiss on her lips but did not respond. A year from now she did not expect to be single, waiting to hear from Jake Macintyre. Even if she was, there was no way she would take his call. All she wanted to do was forget the last twelve hours had ever happened.

Chapter Two

After an entire year away from home, Jake had a severe case of culture shock. Just a few days earlier, he'd been in Tibet, living in a Buddhist monastery. He'd eaten no meat, spoken only rarely, and scrubbed the rough floors by hand. Now he was sitting at his brother Jamie's opulent dining table, where the odor of charred flesh assailed his nostrils.

Jamie poured ruby-red wine into the crystal wineglass in front of him. "I picked up a case of this Merlot the last time I was on the West Coast." He flashed the wicked grin all women loved. "Along with a full-bodied redhead to match."

Uncle Matt threw back his head and laughed. "Eat up, boys. The steak is perfect. Medium-rare."

Jake watched his uncle bring a forkful of meat to his mouth. Its center was a glistening shade of red-black. His stomach clenched as he considered eating the bleeding lump of meat on his own plate. He took a sip of the wine instead, but the tart liquid seemed to expand in his mouth and he had to swallow hard to get it past the lump in his throat. Even the water he gulped from the heavy goblet tasted peculiar, and he imagined invisible contaminants entering his purified body.

Matt speared the steak on Jake's plate with his fork and transferred it to his own. "I think you're jetlagged, boy. Don't worry, you'll be back on your feed in a day or two. Meanwhile, no sense wasting prime beef."

Jake had grown up with Jamie and Matt, and he knew the three Macintyre men had a reputation in Wickham for being typical, taciturn New Englanders. Yet it seemed like since he'd been back, they'd done nothing but talk, talk, talk.

"You're right. I'm exhausted." He rubbed his forehead, where it felt like his brain had swollen and was pushing against his skull. "I think I'll just crash in the den and grab something to eat later."

Although Jamie's apartment, a penthouse with a view of Boston harbor, was decorated in a minimalist, masculine style, his leather sofa would have screamed "decadence" to the monks, and not just because it was covered in animal hide. As Jake sank into the cushions, he smiled, remembering the discomfort of the pallet he'd slept on in the monastery, and the way his body had protested with aches and pains for the first week of his stay. Now everything felt too soft. It didn't keep him from dropping off to sleep within seconds, however.

"We hope to have the results of the strike-vote by the end of the broadcast." The soft, female voice pulling him out of the depths of sleep was familiar. Familiar and seductive.

He forced his eyes open, and eventually focused them on the plasma television screen mounted on the wall. A commercial for a local auto dealer was blaring. He figured out he'd slept for hours, and Jamie had come in to watch the eleven o'clock news — with no concern that it might wake up his brother, of course. Matt would have gone back to Wickham, since it was a weeknight and he started his day at five.

"Will we have another perfect day tomorrow, Ron?" The anchorwoman with the sexy voice finally reappeared. He sat up and rubbed his eyes. Her face was the one that had haunted his dreams as he traveled through Russia, and as he tossed and turned on his monastic pallet in Tibet. It was the face that had made all others unappealing for the last year.

"Violet." He spoke her name out loud, forgetting Jamie was in the room.

His brother laughed from the Eames chair. "So you're not dead, or in a coma. Although I wouldn't have thought Violet Gallagher was your type. As Uncle Matt would say, she looks a bit too much like she just stepped out of a bandbox."

Now that Jake's vision was clear, Violet was gone from the screen again, replaced by Ron and his satellite weather maps. He'd seen her long enough to notice her long dark hair had been cut and reshaped into a formal, sprayed-in-place style, high and tucked behind her ears. Her makeup and jewelry were bold, and her jacket was a bright shade of pink.

"She's much softer in person," he told Jamie. Although she'd been the most beautiful woman at the party, when Jake pictured her — which was more often than he wanted to — it was the way she'd looked the next morning, sleeping beside him, with all traces of self-consciousness gone.

She was in Boston now, and he'd been engaged in a constant debate with himself since he returned. Should he call her? Or should he find someone else, and have the kind of short-term fling he was accustomed to, one that didn't leave him uselessly yearning for more?

"How do you know her?" his brother asked. "I didn't think she started working at Channel Twelve until after you left last June."

"She moved here from Wickham. I went to her going-away party with Uncle Matt the night before I left." As it had so many times, the memory of that night came back to him intact. The soft breeze on the balcony, the tentative kiss that quickly became urgent. The mind-blowing night in Violet's bed. At the airport the next day, he'd even considered staying — until he considered the contracts and lawyers and how unemployable he'd be after stiffing his publisher.

"That's all?"

For the first time in his life, Jake was reluctant to share the intimate details with his brother. "That's all."

"I was worried for a minute. It always seemed like there was something off about the artificial insemination story."

In the past few days, English had sometimes made little sense to Jake, something he'd ascribed to the rapid cultural changes. Although he knew what artificial insemination meant, he couldn't grasp its context here. "You've lost me."

His brother clicked off the television just as Violet reappeared on the screen, and Jake swallowed back a protest.

"*Miss* Gallagher has been on maternity leave for the last three months. Single motherhood isn't unusual these days, but the story is she planned it, picked a sperm donor out of a catalog. She'd just started her new gig, so it doesn't seem likely, does it?"

Jake shrugged. "I don't know her well enough to know what she'd do." He hoped his voice sounded normal, and not as shaky as he was feeling.

Jamie rose and stretched. "Time for me to turn in, I've got a flight to New York in the morning. An opportunity to design a new building in Manhattan. When I get back, you'll get to meet Pamela." His new woman, whom he swore was *the one*.

But Jake had heard that before, and couldn't think about it now. As soon as his brother left the room, he grabbed the remote and brought the oversized screen back to life. Violet was reporting that airline baggage handlers would strike the next day, her face showing concern. He shook his head, trying to clear it. Violet, the sweet enchantress of his dreams, was a mother now. Her baby had been born three months ago. He did the math.

Was the child his? If so, why hadn't she let him know? He could call Richard Rayburn and ask him; when he'd checked his email earlier that afternoon he'd discovered a message from Violet's former co-anchor. He said he'd gotten the cable job in Boston and wanted to do a story on Jake's new book. No, Jake decided, he'd go straight to the one person who was sure to know the answer to his question. His agent, Millie, knew everyone in Boston and he'd bet she could get him the address.

On his way to his room, he opened Jamie's door and stuck his head in. "Go with a carry-on tomorrow. Just a suggestion."

*

When Violet got home at midnight, she was wide awake, jazzed up from caffeine and adrenaline, and yet exhausted to the very core of her being. She'd been tired for three months now. Although the nanny had been living with them for a few weeks, Violet still woke up every time the baby cried, milk soaking the T-shirts she wore to bed.

Her brother Seth was watching television in her living room with a big bowl of popcorn on his lap.

"Where's Carrie?"

"She went to bed right after the news."

"Good. I can have Daisy all to myself when she wakes up for her midnight feeding." She began to strip off her jewelry, beginning with the heavy earrings. They didn't believe in the natural look at Channel 12, and she hadn't been there long enough to feel she could make it an issue.

Seth reached up for her hand and pulled her down on the couch beside him. "Vi, Daisy doesn't wake up for a midnight feeding anymore."

"Of course she does. Last night . . ."

"You woke her up, and all she did was fuss. She wasn't hungry. Carrie just fed her two hours ago."

She took a deep breath, trying to forestall the tears that came so frequently in the past year she'd had to make a permanent switch to waterproof mascara. "I don't think Daisy likes Carrie. She's been so fussy, off her schedule."

Seth moved the popcorn to the coffee table and held her hand in both of his. "Remember, I've been through this already. A baby's schedule changes several times in the first year, something you, the queen of schedules, will just have to learn to accept. She's probably fussy because there's been so much upheaval lately. Carrie coming to live in, you going back to work. She might even be upset because I'm here."

"Daisy loves you! I don't know what either of us would have done without you."

Her tears welled up again. She remembered her frantic phone call to her brother the night she'd finally done the pregnancy test, and how he'd gotten on a redeye flight from California and arrived the next morning. Her period was a month late; she'd already moved to Boston and begun her new job. *We used condoms every time,* she kept telling herself, followed by *life changes are stressful, and stress can make a period late.* Finally, she admitted the truth. The condoms were old, and stress had never made her late in the past.

Once he'd gotten the whole story out of her, Seth had asked, "Mistake or not, you want the baby, don't you?"

She'd nodded, too overcome with emotion to speak. This might be her only chance to be a mother, and she already loved the child growing inside her. Although she'd never considered single motherhood, she was well established in her career and could afford to raise a child on her own. She believed every child should have a father, but she would worry about that later. Jake was not a candidate for the position, that much was clear. Maybe she'd make a new plan — the *father* plan — and find someone mature and responsible. Someone she wouldn't have to call on the French Foreign Legion to locate in an emergency.

"What about the guy? Are you planning to tell him?" Seth had asked her next.

"I don't even know how to find him," she'd replied, although of course Matt Macintyre would know how to reach his nephew. But why bother? "The night this happened he didn't tell *me* he'd be leaving the country the next day, so I don't feel like I owe him anything. And I don't want my child to have a father who's always coming and going, like . . . "

"Monty." Neither of them ever referred to him as Dad. That honor belonged to their stepfather.

Together they'd come up with the idea of telling people single motherhood had been her choice, planned all along. They could believe it or not, but at least no one would ever guess the father's identity. Except possibly Jake Macintyre, and she tried not to think about that. Tried not to think about *him*, and how magical the night of the party had seemed. Or how foolish she'd been to jump into bed with a man she knew nothing about, all because she was in a rush to find her special someone. Ironically, she had — her name was Daisy Gallagher, and Violet couldn't imagine life without her now.

Going back to work had been the most recent crisis, and once again she'd made a tearful phone call to her brother. For the first time in her working career, she hated her job. She just wanted to spend every minute with her baby, nursing her, cuddling her, and gazing into the bright eyes already changing from dark blue to tawny brown. Seth had disrupted his life and come East without a moment's hesitation.

"I'm sorry I took you away from Jenna and Ian," she said now. "I know you need to get back to San Diego." Her sister-in-law was seven months pregnant, and should have her husband home to help her — a luxury Violet didn't have. All she had was the nanny, a young woman who lowered her eyes when Violet spoke to her. Although Carrie was pleasant and competent, their relationship hadn't warmed up in the three weeks she'd been living under her roof.

Seth put his arm around her and blotted her eyes with his handkerchief. "I have a business meeting here tomorrow morning, but I should leave the next day. Will you be all right?"

She sighed. "I'll have to be."

*

Violet nursed Daisy when she woke up at six, then handed her over to Carrie and went back to sleep. She was disappointed when she woke up again a couple hours later to find a note under the sugar bowl saying the nanny had taken the baby for a walk in the park a few blocks away from the townhouse.

She poured herself a cup of the coffee Seth made before he left for his appointment and sat down with the newspaper, but she couldn't concentrate. Why did she need to read the paper, anyway, when she'd be reading the news to all of Boston at six and eleven? She cradled the cup in both hands, and eventually a tear dropped into it and disappeared in the dark liquid. Reporting the news had once seemed all-important to her, but now she couldn't remember why.

Although she knew the baby wasn't there, she followed her urge to go up to the nursery, where she lifted a soft pink blanket from the crib and held it against her face. She breathed in the intoxicating scent she hadn't even known existed until three months ago. Baby. *Her* baby. With the blanket draped over her shoulder, she washed her face and brushed her teeth, then pulled her hair into a short ponytail. She'd had it cut only at her station manager's urging, but had to admit it was easier to manage now that her life was so hectic.

When she heard the doorbell ring, she assumed it was Carrie, needing help with the stroller.

"I'm coming," she called as she ran down the stairs, so anxious to get to her baby that milk began to leak from her breasts. The blanket fell from her shoulder and she tossed it onto a chair in the living room. When she got to the front door, she threw the deadbolt and opened it without checking through the peephole first, something she'd made Carrie swear never to do.

"Oh!" Standing in front of her was Jake Macintyre. Their encounter twelve months earlier had been so brief, she'd often wondered if she'd even recognize him again. She did, in an instant, although he wasn't exactly as she remembered him. He was leaner, paler, and his smile didn't light up his face like it had the night they met. His eyes raked her from top to bottom, and she found herself gripping the top of her short cotton robe, pulling it tighter. One hand went to the stub of her ponytail and she felt her face heat up as she imagined how she must appear to him.

He finally smiled, but the smile didn't reach his steely eyes. "Remember me? Jake Macintyre — you said I could look you up when I got back to Boston."

"Of course! It's just that it was . . . such a long time ago." Not knowing what else to do with her hands, she clutched the sash of her white robe. It hid the last few pounds of baby weight, or at least she hoped it did. She was glad now that Carrie had taken Daisy out and the stroller wasn't in its usual place in the hall, but she needed to get rid of Jake before they returned.

"A year." He removed his hand from the doorframe, moving forward slightly as he readjusted his weight.

Violet, startled, pulled back.

"I'm sorry, am I making you nervous?"

She laughed, and it sounded fake even to her. "Nervous? No, of course not! But I'm not dressed, and I have an appointment . . ."

"What happened to the silk robe you were wearing the last time I saw you? It was pale pink, with a design of water lilies."

The white cotton robe she was wearing had damp spots of leaking milk over her breasts, and she tried to cross her arms over them. "It wasn't . . . practical."

"Probably not. Not for a new mother."

She opened her mouth to protest, but knew it was useless. She was a public figure, and everyone who watched her newscast knew she'd had a baby in March. Anyone could have told Jake. "My baby isn't . . . any of your concern." She'd been planning to say *isn't yours*, but the lie wouldn't pass her lips.

He pushed past her into the hall. "I'd rather not have this conversation on your front step."

She shut the door, first scanning the street for Carrie and Daisy. Maybe she would have to share her daughter with this stranger, this *angry* stranger, but she was hoping desperately for time to think and consider her options first. Seth would help her figure out what to do, if she could just calm Jake down and get him out of there.

"I suppose I should be flattered you picked me," he said when she turned to face him, "but I don't appreciate being used as a sperm donor without my permission. If it isn't illegal, it ought to be."

"*Sperm donor?*" Although it was the story she herself had spread, she was appalled at the man's ego. He thought she'd selected him to be the father of her child. Based on what, his stunning good looks? How shallow did he think she was? "You think I planned my pregnancy."

He crossed his arms over his chest, and an image popped into Violet's memory of his naked body, with its fine blonde hairs scattered over hard, thick muscles. Then she was distracted by the vein jumping at his temple and the fury in his amber eyes.

"Didn't you?" In the face of her anger, he didn't seem quite so sure of his claim.

"Of course not. We used condoms, remember? A bit past their 'use by' date, as I figured out later." She gestured toward the sofa in the living room. "Please, sit down." Although she was still hoping to hurry him out, her legs were shaking and she felt weak.

After a moment's hesitation he sat, rubbing his hands over his eyes and forehead as though he had a headache. She spotted the baby's blanket on the chair across from him and sat on top of it, trying to push it beneath her so he wouldn't see it. It was irrational, she knew, but she was still hoping they could keep the discussion impersonal. Hoping he would give up any claim to Daisy and disappear again, into some jungle on the other side of the world.

"I probably should have told you, but I didn't see any point in disrupting your life, too. We're strangers. Believe me, this was a huge shock to me. But I wanted the baby, and I didn't want — or need — anything from you. That's still the case."

He leaned forward. "At least you had nine months to get used to the idea of being a mother." His gaze went to the seat of her chair, and a corner of the pink blanket that was sticking out behind her. "It's a girl?"

She remembered her doctor saying those same words all those months ago when Daisy was a hazy rolling image on the ultrasound screen. Violet had cried. Not the typical tears of joy, as the doctor and her nurse assumed, although joy was one of the emotions she was feeling. She had cried because she was hearing those words alone.

"Yes. A girl." She pulled the blanket out from beneath her and cradled it protectively in her arms as though it were Daisy herself.

Jake appeared shaken, although she had no idea what the news meant to him. "Where is she?" He scanned the room as though she might be hidden somewhere nearby. "What's her name?"

"She's out with the nanny, and her name is Daisy."

"Daisy?" His eyebrows lifted and his lip curled with the hint of a smile.

"It was my mother's idea, and I told her absolutely not, enough with the flowers. But she looks . . . like a Daisy. It's hard to explain."

He laughed, and with the tension gone from his face, he was once again the charming, handsome man who'd enticed her to break all her rules on a balmy night last June. Dangerously charming — like Monty McCall, who had abandoned her mother and made her childhood miserable.

"I guess I'll have to see for myself." He shook his head. "I can't believe I have a daughter."

Violet needed to do something desperate before he became totally comfortable with the idea of fatherhood. She figuratively crossed her fingers behind her back. "Jake, there's a man in my life. He wants to marry me and adopt Daisy. You'd be doing us all a big favor by walking away. It can be just like it never happened."

What she described was her vision of an ideal future. A few years after her mother and Monty officially divorced, she'd married her widowed boss. David Gallagher was a wonderful man who'd adopted her and Seth, bringing stability to their lives for the first time. Someday, she hoped, she'd walk down a church aisle in a white wedding gown with David at her side to give her away. As for the man waiting at the altar, there were currently no prospects.

Jake jumped up, once again making her shrink back in fear. But he only began to pace. "I don't like this, any of it. A nanny. Some guy adopting my child. It's not right that I have nothing to say about it." He stopped in front of Violet and stared down at her. "I want to see her, at least. I'll get a lawyer if I have to."

If she didn't get him out of the house, immediately, he'd see Daisy whether she agreed to it or not. She stood and walked toward the door, hoping he'd follow. "We'll work something out, Jake. You're right, you should be able to see her if that's what you want. Where can I reach you later tonight?"

While he pulled his wallet out of his back pocket and extracted a business card, she opened the front door, desperately hoping Carrie and Daisy wouldn't be on the other side of it. To her relief, they were nowhere in sight, and Seth was emerging from a cab in front of the townhouse.

"You have twenty-four hours to contact me." Jake handed her the card. "After that, I'm getting a lawyer and taking you to court."

He turned away from her and nearly collided with her brother as he stepped onto the stoop. "Is this the guy?" He turned back to glare at her, rage clouding his eyes.

Before she could answer, he took a step toward Seth and grabbed him by the front of his jacket. "You can't have my daughter."

"Jake, stop! This is my brother."

He relaxed his hold on Seth's jacket, and then looked from his face to Violet's. The twins shared the same striking combination of blue eyes and black hair; no one could doubt their relationship. He let the other man go. "Sorry. I didn't know you had a brother."

Seth clutched his briefcase to his chest. He was speechless and appeared stunned.

"You don't know *anything* about me." Violet was breathing hard, as though she was the one Jake had manhandled. "Please just go."

He glared at her but said nothing, then turned and fled to his car. Just as he peeled away from the curb, she turned in the opposite direction and saw Carrie round the corner with the baby stroller. Bursting into tears, she fell into her brother's arms.

*

"I guess we should have expected this." Seth reached for Daisy, and Violet, who'd been trying to console her for the last fifteen minutes, let him take over. The baby, calm and quiet after her walk, had begun to howl as soon as her tense and sobbing mother snatched her away from the confused nanny.

"Does he have any legal rights?"

Seth began to walk, jiggling Daisy against his shoulder, until the piercing cries stopped. "I'm not an expert on family law, but I know he can try to prove paternity, which would give him rights. From there he could even petition for custody."

"Custody!" Her outburst made the baby wail again.

"Shh, it's okay."

Violet wasn't sure which of them he was speaking to. "It's not okay!"

"It won't come to that," he said in a sing-song voice meant to soothe the baby. "From what you've told me, no judge is going to give him custody of a child, certainly not an infant. I think he just wants to see her."

"And I have to let him." It wasn't a question.

"Let her spit up on him a few times, and he'll run for the hills."

"Like Monty," she said, and he nodded.

"She must be hungry, she's sucking on my shirt." Seth offered the baby back to Violet, who was sitting in the rocking chair he'd given her when Daisy was born.

She tucked the baby inside her robe and spread the pink blanket over them. The creases across Daisy's tiny forehead made her resemble a worried old woman, and Violet took a deep breath, attempting to calm herself so her milk would flow. As she felt it release, Daisy's eyes flew open and sought her mother's. Although she'd known they were losing the blue color they'd had at birth, she realized now they were turning the color of Jake's.

His eyes, softened by lust, had captivated her the night of the party. Today they were cold, full of anger — maybe even loathing. She sniffled, struggling not to cry again while she nursed the baby. It was so unfair, not to mention confusing. Had Jake misled her, or was she the guilty one for jumping into bed with a stranger?

Once she'd felt the first stirrings of her baby inside her, she'd decided guilt and blame did not apply. All that mattered was this exquisite, unexpected child who had come into her world. Had, in fact, become her world.

"We have to protect Daisy, Seth. I'll do whatever I need to do."

Crouching on the floor in front of them, her brother took her hand.

"I know you will."

"Hand me the phone, and I'll call him right now."

Chapter Three

Jake appreciated the natural beauty of every place he visited, whether it was the Himalayas, the Russian steppes, or Boston Commons. As he passed through on his way to meet Richard Rayburn at a trendy restaurant on Charles Street, he practiced the mindfulness meditation the Tibetan monks had taught him. He was a natural at it. When the boys were little, it was only Jamie their mother had to scold to pay attention. Jake was aware of everything.

Right now, everything included the mingled smells of flowers and food, sunlight reflecting off the water, and the shrieks of overexcited children who had come to ride the Swan boats and see the duckling statues. One of his earliest memories was of a ride in a Swan boat with Jamie and both their parents. Although he couldn't picture his father's face, he remembered being lifted in strong arms, and the rumble of his father's laughter deep inside his hard chest.

One day his father hadn't come home from work. Years later Jake would hear the details about the accident, but at the time his red-eyed mother told him only that his father had gone to heaven. Not knowing where heaven was — maybe on the other side of Main Street, which he wasn't allowed to cross? — he'd hoped for a long time to someday find his father's new home.

When the pigtailed toddler in front of him on the path stopped suddenly to sniff a flower, he realized he had strayed from his meditative state. His heart raced as he imagined his own daughter, whom he would meet in two days. Ever since he'd found out about her, his emotions had fluctuated wildly, an unfamiliar state for Jake.

At first he'd been furious at Violet for *getting* pregnant, but then had felt foolish when he realized that, of course, it had been an accident. One she'd had no more control over than he did. Then he'd almost punched her brother's lights outs when he thought he was the man who wanted to adopt the baby — so much for practicing nonviolence. He smiled to himself, picturing the man's startled face. If he got the opportunity, he'd have to apologize.

What would happen now, he wondered? Uncle Matt always told Jake and Jamie a real man did the right thing. Except he didn't know what that *was* in this situation. Violet had moved on, found someone to love — someone more dependable than Jake. So much for the fantasy he'd entertained when Violet held the pink blanket against her chest, that this beautiful woman would now, somehow, *have* to be his. In those few seconds, it had seemed possible. But he knew the solution to his conundrum, if there was one, did not include him and Violet being together.

As soon as his eyes adjusted to the darkness of the restaurant, he spotted Rayburn sitting at the bar. Although his Zen master would have scolded him for the unkind thought, the phrase that came to mind was "fat and happy." Not fat in a literal sense. He just seemed self-satisfied and soft, a man with no hard edges.

He clapped Rayburn on the back. "So you got the job."

The other man smiled and grasped Jake's hand. "It was meant to be."

Jake followed him to their table, only half-listening while the other man described his new job responsibilities and the series of interviews he wanted Jake to do. Once they were seated, Rayburn tried to order him a single-malt whiskey, but he asked for mineral water. He didn't need to read the menu, having already decided on a salad, but Richard concentrated on it like it was a legal contract while Jake, anxious to talk about Violet, played with his fork.

"So, do you see much of Violet Gallagher?" he asked as soon as the other man snapped his menu shut. If the two of them were still friends, he would know the identity of the man who wanted to adopt his daughter.

Rayburn frowned, and didn't reply until they'd given the waiter their order. Then he leaned back in his chair with his arms crossed in front of his charcoal jacket.

"It's you, isn't it? You're Daisy's father. I can't believe I didn't figure it out until now."

Jake couldn't believe it either. He didn't know if the baby resembled him, but couldn't the man do simple arithmetic? "Violet never told you?"

"No. She just said the man wouldn't be part of Daisy's life, and it was what I wanted to hear."

So much for the six months spent in a monastery learning to control his emotions, including anger — Jake's blood was starting to simmer. Again. "I couldn't be part of my daughter's life when I didn't know I *had* a daughter."

Richard's eyes opened so wide the white was visible above the irises. "She didn't tell you, either?"

"Very close-lipped girl, our Violet."

Jake could see the other man felt as foolish as he did, and they shared a rueful smile as the waiter placed their meals in front of them.

"Did you know Violet's father was Monty McCall?" Richard asked when the waiter left.

"The Ultimate's original drummer?"

He nodded, his mouth full.

Jake knew Monty McCall was an over-the-top bad boy rocker who lived the phrase "sex, drugs, and rock-and-roll," and died by it, too.

"Her stepfather adopted Violet and her brother, that's why her name is Gallagher. I suspect that after having some experience with bad parenting, she didn't think an accidental pregnancy would turn you into father of the year."

"But here's the thing," Jake said, ignoring his salad. "Daisy is my child. I can't just let some other guy waltz in and raise her.

Violet needs to give me a chance. Just because my job takes me out of the country doesn't make me Monty McCall."

Richard chewed his salmon slowly and took a sip of wine, frowning at Jake over the rim of the glass. "What other guy?"

"Listen, do you still talk to Violet, or not?" If so, Jake was starting to think the man was as dumb as a stump. "She told me she's getting married, and I want to know the man's name."

Richard's face became even more blank, if possible, then lit up a minute later like the scoreboard at Fenway Park. "She must have meant *me*! I'm always asking her to marry me, and she hasn't said yes yet, but . . ."

"Are you telling me you're not sure?" Jake gripped his fork in his fist.

"I know for a fact she isn't seeing anyone else."

"Do you really know anything about Violet *for a fact*?" Jake slammed the fork down on the table. This clown was going to raise his child?

Richard leaned across the table. "I will tell you just once, Macintyre. I never want to hear you say anything like that again. I've known Violet for five years, and loved her all of them. You spent one night with her. Do you know her favorite food, or favorite color? Did you know she's deathly afraid of spiders, and loves hockey? *You're* the one who doesn't know anything about her."

It was the same thing Violet had said to him, when he was about to smash her brother's face in. Well, he would have to educate himself. He removed some bills from his wallet and tossed them on the table. "That's going to change. She and I have a child to raise — together."

*

Violet wanted everything to be perfect when Jake arrived on Saturday. This time she'd be dressed, which would be a big improvement right there. Daisy would show off her new tricks, bubble-blowing or the laugh that came straight from her round belly, and the townhouse would shine like a spread in a decorating magazine. Jake would see she was an excellent mother, and realize it would be foolish to try for custody. Just in case that thought was on his mind.

What she hadn't counted on was how difficult it would be to pull off this stunt without Carrie there. She usually welcomed having the baby to herself on the weekend, and was still uncomfortable sharing her home with a near-stranger. Although she'd had years of experience at getting people to open up to her, Carrie remained uncommunicative on every subject except Daisy. Even so, by Sunday night Violet was always so worn out from taking care of the baby by herself that she welcomed the nanny back as though Mary Poppins herself had come to rescue them.

An hour before Jake was due to arrive, at ten o'clock Saturday morning, the situation was already veering out of control. Daisy had refused to nurse on her usual schedule, and was napping when she should have been awake. Violet's bedroom was strewn with clothes she'd abandoned in her search for the just-right outfit. It shouldn't be too matronly or too sexy, and it had to fit over her enlarged breasts without calling attention to them.

She finally settled on a summer outfit from last year, capri pants that fit if she left them unbuttoned and a sleeveless cotton blouse in shades of blue and green that complemented her eyes. After pulling her hair back and stroking on some mascara, she was satisfied with the end result. Not glamorous, with her round Irish face, and still carrying a few extra pounds, but good enough for Jake Macintyre, whom she was *not* trying to impress.

Checking her watch, she saw there was just enough time to run down and pick up the baby-clutter in the living room and start a fresh pot of coffee.

Then Daisy began to wail. Amplified by the monitor in Violet's room, it was a horrific sound. She had recently begun to make cooing and babbling sounds when she woke up instead of crying immediately, so the insistent shrieks unnerved Violet. Ever since the night of her going-away party in Wickham, nothing in her life had gone according to plan. Today wasn't going to be an exception.

She ran into the nursery and snatched the baby from her crib. "Daisy, please don't cry. You're about to meet your . . . somebody important, and we want him to think you're a happy baby."

Her words only made Daisy cry harder, so she dropped into the glider to nurse her. She could already feel the pressure of her milk letting down.

Then the doorbell rang.

The word she blurted out was the one she'd banished from her vocabulary when Daisy was born. She stopped crying and stared at her.

"Sure, *that* you pay attention to."

She sped down the stairs, hoping to at least greet Jake before Daisy started crying again.

Peeking first through the peephole this time, she saw him bouncing on his heels and grinning like a boy on his first date. He ran his hand through his short curls. Was he preening for her or for Daisy? Not that it mattered. Neither of them cared.

His gaze locked on the baby in her arms as soon as she answered the door.

"Oh, Violet, she's beautiful!"

At the sound of his voice, Daisy's lips puckered, followed two seconds later by a resumption of the ear-splitting wails.

Jake stepped inside and closed the door behind him. "Is something wrong with her? Is there anything I can do?"

"She's just hungry." Violet hoped that was true, but she was still pretty new to the motherhood thing and wouldn't swear to it. She led him into the living room, where she snatched up baby clothes and diapers from the couch with her free hand. "Have a seat. I'm going to have to feed her."

She tossed the clothes into a corner — so much for the pristine house — and sat in the rocker across from him. When Daisy began to root against her shirt in search of the nipple, they both immediately understood her dilemma. Glancing down, Violet saw two large wet spots on the front of her blouse.

"Would you like me to . . . wait somewhere else?" he asked her, examining his hands.

"Yes. No. I mean, I was going to make coffee, but Daisy didn't sleep when she was supposed to . . . I really just need to go upstairs for a blanket." *And a different shirt.* How had she not grasped the difficulty buttons would present?

He stood up and she followed suit, bouncing Daisy to try to quiet her. "I can make coffee. Just direct me to the kitchen and show me where you keep it. Then you can go upstairs and feed Daisy in private. I'm sure this must be upsetting for her."

Violet almost laughed. Did he think the baby knew who he was and that he had come to disrupt their peaceful life together? Then she realized that it was upsetting for *her* — the thought itself had made her heart rate speed up — and she was surely transmitting that unease to Daisy.

She walked toward the front entry and the stairs, and pointed him toward the kitchen at the back of the townhouse.

"You'll find everything you need in the cabinet above the coffeemaker, and there's a box of pastries on the counter." The pastries she'd run out for that morning, disrupting the baby's schedule and creating the chaos that had led to this uncomfortable moment. She was about to add *make yourself at home,* but stopped herself when she remembered that was the last thing she wanted him to do. "I'll be down in fifteen or twenty minutes."

"Please don't rush on my account. I know that wouldn't be good for Daisy." His smile was wide, as though it pleased him to say her name.

As she settled herself and Daisy in the glider up in the nursery, Violet wondered just how much Jake knew about what was and wasn't good for babies, and how he knew it. When she'd discovered she was pregnant, she'd used every connection she had to get the scoop on Jake. She hadn't learned much. He traveled the world taking photographs for his successful series of books, and apparently traveled light — she'd found no evidence of children or other relationships, other than his brother and uncle. They might share a child, but he was still the mysterious — and attractive, she had to admit — stranger he'd been the night of her going-away party.

Daisy settled into a strong sucking rhythm and gazed up at her with those tiger-yellow eyes. "Like it or not," she said to the baby, "I think we're going to get to know Jake Macintyre a lot better."

*

Thirty minutes later she followed the intoxicating scent of fresh-brewed coffee to the kitchen. She was dressed in a more practical pullover shirt and carrying a much calmer baby. Jake was sitting at the table working on the *Boston Globe* crossword puzzle, a mug of coffee in front of him.

He jumped up when he saw her. "I hope you don't mind?" he asked, gesturing toward the paper. The puzzled was almost completely filled in. In ink.

She laughed. "I don't have time to read it these days, much less do the crossword." If she didn't work for a news station, she'd be a completely ignorant about current events.

"How do you like your coffee?" He was already pouring her a steaming mug.

"Cream and sugar, please."

A minute later he placed her cup on the table, along with the pastries. It surprised her that he'd gone to the trouble to locate a pretty serving plate.

"Just a suggestion, and you're free to say no if you're not ready, but maybe I could hold the baby? You're probably tired of doing everything one-handed."

He shifted his gaze from her eyes to the baby's, and Violet could feel Daisy kicking against her and waving her arms. The tiny traitor smiled at Jake, who was grinning back. His hands were clasped together, as though to stop himself from reaching out before Violet gave the okay.

Feeling like she was four years old again and being forced to share her favorite toy, she nodded her head, blinking back tears. Her arms were empty so fast it seemed like Daisy had jumped into Jake's arms. Into her *father's* arms.

Violet dropped into the chair Jake had pulled out for her and took a big sip of coffee, burning her mouth. "Too hot." She pretended that was the reason her eyes were watering.

Jake paid no attention, and neither did Daisy, for that matter. He was sitting and holding her in the crook of his arm, telling her what a beautiful girl she was, getting immodest smiles and happy gurgles in return. He appeared totally comfortable with a baby in his arms. Much more comfortable, in fact, than Violet had been the first time she held her. Once again she was reminded of how little she knew about this man.

"You've had some experience with babies."

He tore his gaze away from Daisy and turned it back to Violet. "The family I stayed with in South Africa had twins, and I gave the mother a helping hand whenever I could." He flipped the baby onto his shoulder. "I think she's ready to be burped."

Violet remembered what Seth had said about Jake running the first time the baby spit up on him, but it was obvious it would take more than that to get rid of this man. Taking pity on him, she got up and grabbed the dish towel, and placed it under Daisy's nestled head.

"Thanks." He turned his head and smiled at her, and she realized her hand had lingered a moment too long, until she was aware of the heat of his skin beneath the soft cotton of his shirt.

She immediately moved her hand to Daisy's head, and caressed her silky hair.

"What a beautiful shirt. Something you got on your travels?" She returned to her chair and sipped her coffee, which had cooled.

He laughed. "In my travels through Quincy Market, yesterday. I lost weight from the vegetarian diet in Tibet, and all my American clothes are too big."

Violet had noticed he was leaner; his jaw and cheekbones were more chiseled, in a male model sort of way. But, if anything, his body seemed even more muscular, more powerful. She dropped her eyes, feeling a blush rise up her neck as she imagined his body naked. What was wrong with her? This man was the enemy.

Daisy burped in response to Jake's gentle patting, and milk trickled from her mouth onto the towel. He blotted her pouting lips but seemed unfazed.

"She's falling asleep," Violet said. "I'm afraid she's totally off her schedule."

"Schedules are an American concept."

"Well, we're Americans." *Here we go.* He was going to tell her how to raise her baby, even though he'd be running off to some foreign country in a few months. "I should put her in the crib."

She stood and reached for Daisy, but Jake just held her more tightly against his chest. Her arms returned to her sides, where her hands clenched into trembling fists. He was the preschool bully who wouldn't give her back her doll, and Violet felt a familiar surge of fury and frustration. She wasn't a helpless four-year-old, she reminded herself, and she didn't have to let Jake Macintyre push her around; she'd let him know who was in charge here. But Jake spoke before she could form the words.

"I'm sorry." He eased the sleeping baby off his shoulder and cradled her on his lap. "You know what's best for Daisy. It just feels so good to hold her. Can I at least carry her upstairs to her crib?"

Violet's hands uncurled. Daisy wasn't supposed to be napping now and probably wouldn't sleep long. Jake wasn't trying to challenge her authority, he just wanted more time with the baby.

"Why don't you hold her in the rocker, where you can both be more comfortable? I brought a blanket down."

"Thank you." He held her eyes, and for the first time, aimed his hundred watt smile directly at her instead of the baby.

It was the smile she remembered from the night of her going-away party. The one that had made her feel all warm and tingly, although not as tingly as she felt when his hand first touched the bare skin of her back, or when he kissed her on the patio. Or when he . . . she shook her head, reminding herself, as she had so many times, that she'd had too much champagne that night. If she wanted to feel a tingly sensation again, all she had to do was open a bottle of bubbly. It might not be quite the same, but it was certainly safer.

She shrugged and turned away. "I'll pour us more coffee. How do you take yours?"

"Black." He stood and moved the baby to his shoulder in one easy motion. "I had no coffee, meat, caffeine, or sugar for the six months I was in Tibet. I'm taking up the Western vices again one by one, but I haven't wanted sugar yet."

That would explain why he hadn't taken one of the pastries she'd gone out for this morning. She'd eaten two before he arrived. "You consider delicious food to be a vice?"

Her tone was sharper than she'd meant it to be, and he held his free hand up, palm out, as though to ward her off. "Don't shoot me, I didn't mean it as a criticism. It was hard to give those things up, but when I did I felt pure, healthier. My brain felt sharp and clear, and I think my work was the best I've ever done."

Violet stopped herself from reaching for the lemon Danish. "My brain hasn't felt sharp in a year." She felt like she was sleepwalking her way through her workday, but still felt like she's climbed a mountain when she left the studio each night.

"That's from hormones, and lack of sleep. I don't think sugar or any other food is evil, and I'm sure I'll eat it again someday. I tend to get fired up about the new things I discover when I travel, then move on just as wholeheartedly to the next thing."

He smiled again, then turned and headed to the living room. This time Jake's boyish grin reminded Violet of Monty, which made her feel warm in a different way. She followed him, and set his coffee cup on the side table next to the rocker so hard it sloshed.

"Is that what my baby is to you? The 'next thing'?" she asked, standing over him.

"What?" Daisy startled at the sound of his voice, and he soothed her with a hand on the back of her head.

"When you go back on the road, you'll forget all about us." She was flustered. Had she just said *us*? "I mean, you'll forget about Daisy."

He sighed. "Violet, please sit down. I can't think with you looming over me."

She sank onto the sofa and tried to take deep breaths. "I don't want you popping in and out of my daughter's life. She needs a father she can depend on."

"Like Rayburn, I suppose?" He pushed the rocker into warp speed.

Now Violet was confused, by his angry tone as much as the name. "Richard? What does he have to do with this?"

Daisy stirred again, and he slowed the rhythm of the rocker. "I had lunch with him yesterday. I know he's the man you're planning to marry. Personally, I think you could do a lot better."

Violet's sleep-deprived brain finally came through with the missing information — she'd told Jake there was a man in her life who wanted to marry her. Now that she thought about it, it was true. Richard *did* want to marry her, and had mentioned several times that he'd like to adopt Daisy. But she'd always made light of his proposals and changed the subject. How could Richard think she was going to marry him? Of course the important thing was that *Jake* believed it.

"Who I marry is none of your business."

"Violet, the man is a buffoon!"

"He's a wonderful man. Daisy couldn't have a better father."

Richard was, she had to admit, the most loyal and dependable friend she had. He was intelligent and honest, a man cut from the same mold as her stepfather, David Gallagher. Most importantly, he was always there when she needed him. The only problem was he didn't make her feel the thrill of desire she'd felt when she met Jake. But was that really so important? After all, she currently had no love life at all, and was resigned to it.

Perhaps because he'd pushed the rocker into an agitated motion once again, or because their voices had risen, Daisy raised her head, scowled at Jake and began to wail. As soon as his first attempts to soothe her failed, it was obvious he wouldn't be able to calm her down. Although Violet wasn't proud of it, she was glad. This time when she stood and held her arms out, he surrendered the baby without protest.

Daisy, relieved to see her mother's face, stopped crying almost at once.

"Then it's true? Rayburn's the guy?"

Violet almost wished the baby would start to cry again so she could delay her response. She patted her back and the baby let out a loud burp — no reprieve. Telling herself the lie was necessary, she mentally crossed her fingers. "Yes. I'm going to marry Richard Rayburn."

Chapter Four

"When?" A vein jumped on Jake's right temple.

Violet shrugged. "We haven't set a date." At least that wasn't a lie. But she needed to change the subject before his temper flared again. "I think Daisy's ready for some playtime now that she's calmed down."

She pulled the play mat from behind and end table and arranged the baby on her back beneath its hanging toys. Daisy gurgled and kicked her feet, setting the toys into motion. As Violet hoped, this distracted Jake from the subject of Richard. He got down on the floor with them and watched, enraptured, as Daisy flailed at the dangling objects.

"I'm probably biased, but she seems advanced for a three-month-old."

"Oh, she is." She knew every mother thought her child was above-average, but the well-thumbed book on child development she kept on the coffee table verified it.

"Does the nanny know she should interact with her like this?"

Violet hesitated. "I tell her, but . . ."

"Where did you find her, anyway? Did you check into her background before you hired her?"

Her first impulse was to ask him if he thought she was a complete idiot, but she bit back the words and took a deep breath before she spoke. After all, he didn't really know much about her, did he? Other than what she looked and felt like naked, and how uninhibited she became when she had too much to drink. She reddened at the thought.

"The agency I used does background checks, of course. But I admit I'm concerned about Carrie."

Daisy had her hand curled around Jake's index finger, and she was gazing into his eyes and vocalizing. It took a minute for what Violet said to penetrate, but then she had his full attention.

"What do you mean?" Daisy responded to the withdrawal of eye contact by dropping his finger and shifting her attention to a bouncing teddy bear.

Violet shrugged. Her intuition was screaming that something was wrong, but she'd always lived her life according to what she *knew*, not what she sensed, and she had no facts to back up her feeling. Would Jake understand, or dismiss her concerns the way Seth and Richard had? Her brother said she was projecting her desire to stay home with the baby into the situation, and maybe he was right.

"It's nothing tangible. Daisy doesn't seem very happy when she's with her, but it could just be that she prefers me."

Jake frowned. "Try to describe how Daisy acts," he said, surprising her.

"A minute ago she reached for your finger and held it. She's trying to make eye contact with you, and she never saw you before today. She doesn't do that with Carrie."

"Does she hold her body rigid when Carrie picks her up?"

"Yes!" Although she hadn't been conscious of it, Daisy's body language was probably the source of her intuition. "But that isn't enough reason to fire someone, is it? Beside, it would take time to interview and hire someone else, and I can't miss more work."

"Have you heard of a nanny-cam?"

"I did a story on them once. They're legal, but it didn't seem ethical to me to spy on someone who works for you. But that was before I had Daisy. I'd do anything to protect her." She smiled at the baby, and the smile she gave in response contorted her whole body. Had she ever seen Daisy smile at Carrie? She'd never heard her laugh when the two were together.

"I'm a big believer in intuition," Jake said, "but if you want evidence before you send the woman packing, I can set up some cameras for you."

Violet hesitated. She'd planned, for her sake and Daisy's, to keep their contact with Jake to a minimum — Saturday mornings only. But her options for dealing with the nanny were limited. She could ask the agency to replace her, but if there was really a problem, she didn't want to just pass her on to another family. Jake was going to be in Boston for a few months in any case, she might as well let him help her.

"Do it," she said to him. "Can you set the cameras up tomorrow afternoon? Carrie will be back at six."

*

After making a stop to discuss his options for the video surveillance of the nanny with a videographer he knew, Jake headed over to the home security store the man recommended. His purchases included a teddy bear with a camera hidden in its belly. As it was being rung up, it struck Jake that he hadn't bought anything for his daughter yet.

Not that Daisy needed more toys. They would probably have to discard a real stuffed animal just to make room for this one on the shelf. He'd walked through the townhouse with Violet before he left, to determine where the cameras should be. Daisy's room was crammed with toys, books, blankets, and frilly pink clothes. The other rooms contained the overflow. When he commented on the abundance, Violet told him her family and coworkers had given her three baby showers. *His* family and friends didn't even know Daisy existed.

He wasn't angry anymore; he understood why Violet hadn't tried to contact him. She was right that becoming a father wouldn't have been at the top of his to-do list, if he kept such a thing instead of pursuing whatever adventure presented itself. But Daisy was here, and she had his eyes. She had his *father's* eyes. Jake hadn't gotten the opportunity to help transport the shower gifts, or time Violet's contractions, or hand out "it's a girl" cigars to Jamie and Matt.

He wouldn't force himself on Violet, but he wasn't going to abandon his flesh and blood — or let himself be driven away. The most important gift he had to give her was her family, and he was going to begin by letting his brother know right now that he had a beautiful niece. Telling him would make it seem more real and his link to Daisy would become irrevocable.

The stereo in the den played soft jazz when he entered Jamie's apartment, and he began speaking as he headed down the hall. "Big brother, you're not going to believe my news."

But when he walked through the door and saw Jamie with a curvaceous blonde woman on his lap, and his hand under the hem of her hiked-up dress, he almost walked right back out.

"Jake! Don't go." The woman giggled as Jamie stood and called to his brother, nearly toppling her to the floor in the process. Not that she could have fallen; she appeared to be glued to his brother's body. "We've been waiting for you. I want you to meet Pamela."

Jamie had told him there was a new woman in his life, a serious woman from the sound of it. His brother had asked her to move in, something he'd never done before. Although he hadn't told Jake he couldn't stay, he planned to move out as soon as he found a place to go. He planned to be in Boston for at least three months, and three would be a crowd for that length of time, no matter how spacious the digs. Not that he expected Jamie's new romance to last. The record was counted in weeks, not months.

"This is my brother, Jake." Without taking his eyes off her, he said, "I've been waiting for Pamela all my life."

Jake hoped Pamela didn't think his brother meant that literally, or she was going to be very surprised when the evidence of all Jamie's ex-girlfriends began to surface. Nearly every day he discovered some of it himself, everything from exotic beauty products in the guest medicine cabinet to thong panties between the cushions on the leather couch.

"Pleased to meet you." It was easy to smile as he imagined her making a similar archeological find.

"You and Jamie have the same beautiful smile."

Her handshake was surprisingly firm, and he remembered she was a successful businesswoman, the decorator who had earned a substantial payday turning Jamie's penthouse into a masculine sanctuary. He wondered how soon the feminine touches would start showing up, or if his brother would be paying for a complete decorating makeover.

"C'mon, we were just going to throw some lunch together." Jamie reached for Pamela's hand and pulled her behind him toward the kitchen. Jake trailed after them, already feeling extraneous. Soon, maybe before she left today, she'd be evaluating him the same way she'd examine the sofa cushions and drapes. Stay, or go? Sorry, the brother has to go, he doesn't match the decor.

The lunch they were "throwing together" had obviously been purchased at an expensive deli. Pamela pulled trays of rich delicacies from the refrigerator, including smoked salmon, pâté, and caviar. He avoided the meat and seafood and filled a plate with marinated baby vegetables, hummus, and over-processed bread with all its nutrition removed. Was this the sort of food Violet would feed Daisy after she weaned her from the breast? He shuddered, and he wasn't sure which thought had caused it — Daisy eating a bad Western diet or Violet's breast.

"Your brother told me you're a vegetarian, but you'll eat some salmon and caviar, right?" Pamela reached past him for the bread and gave him a good view of her own cleavage, suspiciously cavernous for such a slight woman.

Why did Americans have to tweak everything? From the food they ate and the places they lived to their very flesh, nothing was left natural. He pictured Violet opening her door to him the other day in her milk-stained cotton robe, her glossy dark hair pulled back and her face free of make-up. He'd never seen anything as beautiful, despite his anger at her, and he'd seen a lot of amazing sights.

"Maybe later," he told Pamela. He'd learned it was best not to challenge the natives about their eating habits.

"Join me in a beer?" Jamie poured the glass before Jake could answer, so he accepted it without comment. "So, what's your big news?"

"News?" He was eyeing the beer, which was the same dark amber as Daisy's eyes, and thinking it would be refreshing to take a nice, long swallow. Not to mention a good delaying tactic. So he did. When he set the glass back down on the table, with the rich, bitter taste lingering on his tongue, he saw Jamie and Pamela were both waiting for him to speak. He finally had his brother's full attention, but something made him hold back from making his announcement in Pamela's presence.

"Oh, no big deal. My publisher called to tell me they ordered another printing of the last book, and he expects the next one to outsell all the others."

Jamie shot him a questioning look, perfect eyebrows raised, probably because Jake rarely discussed his finances or his career successes. He reached across the table to slap him a high-five when Jake didn't say anything more. "Mom and Dad would have been really proud of you, bro!"

"It sounds like you'll be able to get your own penthouse." Pamela's smile was all innocence. "I can recommend a great decorator."

Nice touch. Get rid of the brother, and make a big commission at the same time.

"I'm not interested in owning any property." Because he wasn't used to alcohol, the beer was already starting to spread warmth to his extremities and soften the hard edges of things, but he could see more would be needed to get through this lunch. He tipped the glass up while Jamie explained him to Pamela.

"Jake's the kind of guy who keeps his boots by the door and his carry-on packed, and he always has been. He just rents my guest room for a few months once a year or so."

Before he could tell Jamie he was planning to make other living arrangements, his brother brought up a new subject.

"Honey, I forgot to tell you my brother knows that anchorwoman, the one named after a flower. Verbena?"

"Violet," he corrected.

Pamela turned her too-white smile on him. He'd been fighting the impulse to stare at people's teeth ever since he returned from Tibet; apparently a new craze had everyone bleaching their teeth to blinding brightness.

"You know Violet Gallagher? I was hired by her station to decorate her townhouse when she first moved to Boston, but it didn't work out." The laughter she tacked on to the end of every statement was starting to annoy him. Hadn't Jamie noticed it?

He shrugged. "As I told Jamie, I just met her once at a party." He shot his brother a warning glance, which he ignored. As usual.

"I was afraid my little bro was the father of her child."

Jake drained the rest of his beer while the other two laughed at Jamie's comment, and jumped up to get another one from the refrigerator.

"No," Pamela said. "I know who the father is."

"How would you know that?" Jake asked without thinking.

She was oblivious to the reproach in his voice and continued blithely on, her eyes sparkling in a way they hadn't until now. He added gossiping to the growing list of her faults.

"Well, she wanted to do her own decorating, and I can only imagine how it turned out! But I went to her townhouse for two consultations, and both times there was a man staying with her. He said he lived in California, and I heard him on the phone talking to his wife. One of those bicoastal guys. I suspected she was pregnant even then, and of course a couple months later it was public knowledge. I got a good laugh out of that trumped-up story about a sperm donor."

Jake returned the unopened beer to Jamie's fridge. He'd need something much higher octane than beer to tolerate Pamela.

"Tell me, did the lawyer from California look a lot like Violet?"

She appeared to think about it, but instead of her brow wrinkling in concentration like a normal person's, her eyes just got wider. Botox?

"They both had the same really dark hair, I guess, and blue eyes. Why?"

"Because that was her brother. Not the father of her child." He headed for the hallway, and turned around when he reached the doorway. "And one more thing. Her townhouse looks great."

He was almost to the elevator when he heard his brother behind him.

"Jake? What just happened? Where are you going?"

He'd like to go back to Tibet. That might be just about far enough away from Pamela, and people like her. But he'd miss the chance to get to know Daisy, to hold her chubby hand while she learned to walk, and hear her say "dada" for the first time. But he was going to miss all those things anyway. He'd be — where? He couldn't even remember. Someplace with beautiful scenery, where he'd take pictures of native women holding their babies and be haunted by visions of Violet and Daisy.

"Just grabbing my boots. They're right here by the door."

*

Jake had said he'd arrive midmorning on Sunday so he'd have plenty of time to set up the cameras before Carrie came home, but this time Violet didn't stress about pastries, Daisy's schedule, or what to wear. She might have to share her child with Jake Macintyre, but she didn't have to act like a foolish schoolgirl in his presence. Until she opened the door and saw him. His tousled curly hair and sleepy-looking eyes made her think he'd just gotten out of bed. "Jake" and "bed" in the same thought made heat rise to her face.

"I hope you have coffee." Oblivious to her flushed face, he dumped a stack of boxes in her foyer and headed for the kitchen. He took a mug from the cupboard as casually as if he'd lived there for years.

"Help yourself." Her teasing was good natured. She still couldn't take her eyes off him as he reached for the cup and poured the coffee, his muscles rippling visibly under his wrinkled white T-shirt. "Did you have a rough night?"

He sipped the steaming brew, finally peering at her over the brim of the cup. "Ah, I needed that. I slept in an unfamiliar bed. You know how that can be."

More sarcastic remarks came to mind, none of them good natured now. But if Jake Macintyre had spent last night in another woman's bed, what was it to her? "With all the traveling you do, I'd think you'd get used to that."

He'd probably slept with women in strange beds all over the world in the past twelve months, while she grew to the size of a circus fat lady with his child inside her. The thought had not escaped her while she was pushing what felt like a small car out of her body.

"I do, but only after a few days. Say, where's my girl?"

"Napping. She won't be up for another forty-five minutes." She poured herself a cup of coffee too, although it would be her third of the morning. "We were up at six. I'm sure I'd have no trouble at all sleeping in a strange bed, or even on a rock."

"Done it," he said, flashing his twinkling smile. "I'll get started down here. I have two cameras for the nursery and one for the living room."

"Can I help?" She followed him back to the front hall, where he pulled a couple boxes off the pile.

"Do you have a set of tools?"

"Just the basics. I bought safety latches to install on my cabinets and I was planning to have Seth or Richard install them for me." She opened the front closet and took out the still-unopened toolbox.

"These will do. I can do the childproofing stuff too, but I might have to stay for lunch. I saw an Indian place down the street where I can get takeout. Do you like curry?"

"Lunch?" She hadn't expected him to stay more than a couple hours, and eating together seemed so . . . intimate. Then she realized she was back to her foolish thoughts and behavior of the previous day. She'd given birth to the man's baby after having the best sex of her life with him, but they couldn't share a meal from a cardboard container?

He grinned. "The meal between breakfast and dinner?"

"Curry would be great." She didn't tell him she had the restaurant's number on her speed dial, assigned to the number three. Only because the pizza place was number two, and number one was assigned to her mother. She loved to cook, even just for herself, and dinner parties were her favorite way to entertain. But the last party she could remember had taken place in her Wickham apartment.

Jake set up the cameras while Violet cleaned in the kitchen and picked up baby clothes and toys. Even when he wasn't in her immediate proximity she was constantly aware of him, and not sure how she felt about having this man in her house. She'd never lived with a man, but had imagined how it would be. Sometimes absorbed in his own interests, but with a spark of connection always between them — the way her mother and David Gallagher were together. She turned her head and their eyes caught and held for a moment before he returned to his task.

He was here because of Daisy, she knew that, but what about the attraction he'd felt to her last year? Was it completely gone? She caught sight of herself in the mirror over the mantel and almost laughed. The difference between her appearance the night of her party last June and now was like comparing Cinderella the night of the ball to one of her ugly stepsisters — or maybe even her step*mother*.

Less than an hour later they heard Daisy "talking" over the baby monitor and she went up to get her. When she reached the bottom of the stairs with the baby in her arms, Jake was removing a teddy bear with a big red bow from one of the boxes. Daisy started to kick and reach for the toy.

Jake laughed. "I'm sorry, sweetie, but this isn't a present. It's a special teddy bear designed to hold a spy camera. It will sit on a shelf in your bookcase and tell us all your secrets."

"I plan to leave it there until she goes to college." Violet distracted the baby with a bright pink teething ring, which Daisy got to her mouth on the third try.

"I do want to do something, though," Jake said as he flattened the empty boxes, "but I need to speak to my lawyer first."

Violet involuntarily tightened her hold on Daisy when she heard the word "lawyer," making her whimper and drop her toy.

Jake reached for the baby, and she held out her dimpled arms to him. Violet, however, was physically unable to let her go. "Your lawyer?"

He sighed and let his arms drop to his sides. "Violet, I know you'd like me to just disappear, but that isn't going to happen. I'm Daisy's father, and that means something to me. The least I can do is make sure she's taken care of financially. I'm going to talk to my lawyer about setting up a trust fund."

"Daisy doesn't need your money."

"I know you have a high-paying career right now, but I want to be sure you and Daisy will always be taken care of, even if something unexpected happens."

There was a time when Violet believed she could control her destiny, then a pink pregnancy test stick had changed her thinking. But when she decided to become a single mother, she'd vowed she would do it on her own.

Daisy was still flirting with Jake, and he wasn't — at least right now — suing her for custody, so she handed the baby to him. She had to give him some credit for at least trying to do the right thing.

"Jake, my father, my biological father, was. . ."

"Monty McCall. Richard told me."

"When I was a kid, we didn't have any money. I didn't have a father, either. Monty — he actually made us call him that, can you believe it? — popped in at odd times that never coincided with our birthday or holidays and showered us with gifts. Even when he started to make money, he never remembered to pay the child support, and my mother was too proud to force him. I had the world's fanciest bride doll, but my shoes were too tight. Still, I'd have rather had a father in my life than comfortable shoes."

The baby was starting to squirm, because Jake was ignoring her and frowning at her mother.

"Violet, I'm not Monty McCall. I want to be part of Daisy's life. You're the one telling me to go away."

She realized her hands were clenched into fists. "A child should have stability. Can you give her that?"

He sighed. "I don't know *what* I can give her yet. You've had a year to decide what kind of father I would or wouldn't be, even though you know almost nothing about me. But because you thought it best to keep me in the dark, I've only had a few days to think about it."

Daisy was fussing now, and Violet took her from Jake. "She's hungry."

During the exchange, he pressed his hand against the skin of her upper arm. She was sure he could feel her trembling.

"I'm just asking you to give me a fair chance. Get to know me before you tell me I'm not good enough to be Daisy's father."

She realized then why she was trembling. She was afraid. It might be easier to hate Jake, or at least dismiss him, if she *didn't* get to know him better. Daisy's eyelashes were darkened by tears, and so were Jake's.

It took a tremendous effort of will to give the answer she knew he deserved. "I'll try."

Chapter Five

"We'll be able to see the main areas of the nursery — the changing table and crib — and the entire living room. Enough of the foyer is captured to show us if she lets anyone in." Jake showed Violet the camera he'd placed in her living room bookcase, disguised as an ordinary book.

"I told her she can never have anyone over when she's here alone with Daisy!"

"Exactly."

Violet wrinkled her brow. "I wasn't thinking anything truly awful was going on, but I suppose you never know."

They gazed at Daisy, in Violet's arms, and Jake placed his hand on her downy head. He was close enough for her to smell his soap. Or the soap belonging to the woman he'd spent the night with, although there was nothing feminine about the way Jake smelled.

"Don't worry," he said, his voice husky. "We'll make sure nothing happens to our girl. Now, where's the hardware that's going to keep her from swallowing drain cleaner?"

The words "our girl" caused a lump to form in Violet's throat. She knew having a husband and partner couldn't guarantee Daisy's safety, but sometimes it just seemed like too big an undertaking for one person to handle alone. Not sometimes — all the time. She handed Jake the shopping bag from the baby store containing every safety device they sold. "Cabinet and drawer latches, outlet plugs, and toilet lid locks so she won't drown."

"In the toilet? Do you know how many places in the world don't even have indoor plumbing?"

"No, but I won't be visiting any of them. And hearing about them all the time could really get on a person's nerves." Especially when that person had once dreamed of becoming a journalist who traveled to all those foreign destinations. The expression of horror on her mother's face when she'd shared that dream had made her lock it away. Now, of course, there was Daisy to consider. Orlando, Florida would probably be her most exotic destination for the next two decades.

He laughed. "I probably talk too much about the places I've been . . ."

"The lock will keep her from flushing away her toys and reduce my plumbing repair bills." Violet also didn't think she'd be able to give Jake the fair chance he'd asked for if she was constantly reminded of his wanderlust. "Why don't I order our lunch while you do that. Vegetarian dishes, right?"

He grinned. "I don't mind if you want to eat something with meat."

So the carcinogens would kill her and he could have custody of Daisy? She ordered three vegetarian dishes just to be on the safe side, then stuffed the rest of yesterday's pastries down the garbage disposal.

Jake installed a few of the latches, then left to pick up their food. Ten minutes later the doorbell rang, and Violet stowed Daisy in her baby seat under the play gym before going to let him in.

"That was fast . . . Richard!"

A very unexpected Richard Rayburn was standing on her front step. In his white pants, cream polo shirt, and deck shoes, he might have just stepped out of the pages of a yachting magazine. His thick hair gleamed with styling gel, and the scent of that and his cologne competed with the bouquet of yellow roses he was holding.

"What are you doing here?"

Richard stuck out his lower lip like a pouting teenager, but before she could smooth over her rudeness, Jake's car pulled up to the curb.

"What's *he* doing here?" Richard asked when he turned and saw him coming up the sidewalk carrying the bag of food.

"Well, he's, Jake is . . ."

"I know he's Daisy father. But I don't see any reason for him to be hanging around, horning in on our time together."

Our time together? Violet wanted to slam the door shut on both men. Sure, they might bang on it and call her name for a while, but eventually they'd go away, right?

"What are you doing here, Rayburn? Did you win the top prize, or just Miss Congeniality?" Jake shoved past Richard and strode back to the kitchen, leaving the other man sputtering.

"What's that supposed to mean, Macintyre?" he yelled after him.

"Richard, come inside." Violet stepped aside for him to pass and closed the door. A quick glance at Daisy in the living room showed she was preoccupied with batting her hanging toys. "Jake is here to install a nanny-cam system for me, and child-safety latches."

"For Pete's sake, Violet, why don't you just fire that woman if you're worried about her? And I was going to install the latches for you." His mellow anchorman voice trailed off into an unpleasant whine.

They followed Jake to the kitchen, where he was pulling plates out of the cupboard. Two plates.

Richard's jaw fell open. "Is he living here?"

"No, of course not."

Jake set the plates on the table, then opened the cabinet over the refrigerator and got down a vase. "You might want to put those in water," he said to Richard. "They're real, right?"

Richard shot her an accusing look, and she made a mental note to ask Jake later how he knew where she kept her vases.

"We agreed Jake can visit Daisy every Saturday."

"But today is Sunday."

The whine in Richard's voice was getting as annoying as Jake's stories about how the rest of the world lived. She took another plate from the cupboard and set it on the table with the others. "Join us for lunch, Richard, we have plenty."

He walked closer to the table and examined the containers Jake was opening, his face twisting into a suspicious grimace. "What is that?"

"Curry," Jake replied, "and there's no meat."

"No meat? What kind of a man doesn't eat meat?"

"I wasn't always a vegetarian. I've eaten meat you've never even heard of, Rayburn. Once when I was in Australia, I ate the eyes and brain of a . . ."

"Jake! Please don't go there, I beg you." A throbbing started over Violet's right eye, something that only happened when she was very tired, or very stressed. Right now she was both. She sank into one of the chairs and rubbed her temples.

Jake spooned vegetables onto her plate, but she'd lost her appetite. Daisy whimpered in the other room. She stood to go to her, but found her way blocked by both men, who were, if she could believe her eyes, shoving each other.

"I'll go, I'm her father."

"Oh, yeah? I held Daisy in the hospital the day after she was born. Where were you then, Macintyre?"

"Freeze!" Violet's command made both men and Daisy all fall silent. "I'll take care of the baby, because I'm the only adult here. You two should leave, and not come back until you can behave."

She went into the other room and picked up the baby, who had resumed her crying at an even higher decibel level. When she returned to the kitchen, neither man had moved.

"And one more thing. If you're ever both in my house at the same time again, God forbid, you're to call each other by your first names."

She was halfway up the stairs when she heard them laughing, but she'd rather die an old maid than go back down and deal with them.

*

It wasn't until his editor reprimanded him about it at their Wednesday morning meeting that Jake even remembered he *had* a cell phone. "I left a message at your brother's. He called me back and said he didn't know where you were."

He dug into his backpack and found the flip phone. Of course its battery was dead. "Sorry. I've been staying at a hotel the last few days."

Mark glared at him. He was used to Jake being unavailable when he was out of the country, but expected him to be accessible when he was in Boston. "Nice of you to share that information with me."

There were seventeen messages on the phone. A quick glance showed that most of them were from Jamie, Mark, or Millie, his agent. He'd have to deal with them later. Right now, he had to get to Violet's while there was still time to review the nanny-cam recordings before Carrie returned from her half-day off.

"I promise I'll leave my cell phone on," he told his editor as he stuffed the folders he'd given him into his backpack.

"And charged!" Mark yelled after him.

*

"How long do we have?" Jake asked Violet when she opened her door twenty minutes later.

"At least two hours. I gave Carrie extra time so she could see her eye doctor. Somehow she managed to walk into an open cabinet door yesterday, and today her eye is swollen and bruised. On top of all that, she came back from her weekend off with a cold, and I'm afraid Daisy will catch it."

Daisy was still taking her morning nap, so Jake started by removing the memory card from the camera he had planted in the living room.

"Jake, there's something I want to ask you."

Her tone was so serious that he turned away from the camera to examine her face. The expression on it was equally grave. Had she changed her mind about letting him see Daisy? Although he would fight her if she did, his heart sank at the prospect of the two of them becoming adversaries.

"Go ahead."

"How did you know where I kept the vases?"

The vases? That was all? He laughed and returned to his work. "Everyone keeps their vases in the cabinet over the refrigerator."

He'd made an educated guess, knowing if he was right it would make Rayburn think he was at least a regular visitor to Violet's townhouse. Remembering the other man's enraged reaction to his stunt made him smile. He didn't want Rayburn to be Daisy's father, and, if he admitted the truth, he didn't want him to be Violet's husband, or even her lover, either. Jake was a keen observer of body language, and he'd bet that the only place Rayburn had been Violet's lover so far was in his dreams.

At least until he and Violet had a chance to get to know each other better, he'd do whatever it took to keep it that way.

They heard a yawn over the baby monitor, and then Daisy's babbling. He followed Violet up the stairs, enjoying the view of her legs in denim shorts. When they got to the nursery, he walked in first and was greeted by Daisy's whole-body grin when he spoke her name.

By the time Violet had the baby changed, his laptop was up and running on the coffee table. They sat side-by-side on the sofa and waited to see the first motion the camera had detected on Monday morning. Daisy stirred, and Violet, wearing a white nightgown, appeared within moments to pick her up.

"The two of you could be an ad for something," he said to Violet. "Baby products, or maybe shampoo." He watched as Violet settled in the glider with Daisy and began to undo the buttons at her bodice.

"Umm, fast forward, please."

He did, trying to hide his grin.

In the next segment, Carrie placed the baby in her crib at naptime. Forty-five minutes later Daisy made the same small waking-up movements as she had at the beginning of the recording, but no one appeared until it was obvious she was in full-blown distress, crying and thrashing.

"Where is she?" Violet put her hands to her face as though she wanted to cover her eyes. Tears were visible on the baby's face.

Finally the nanny appeared, holding a cell phone to her ear. She pinned it against her shoulder just long enough to pick up the screaming baby, then held her awkwardly with one arm. Although they couldn't hear what she was saying, it was apparent from her facial contortions that it was an unpleasant conversation. Then she disappeared from view, and the screen turned to snow.

When it began again, the time display said it was an hour later. Carrie — minus the phone this time — walked into the nursery and placed the baby on the changing table, where she proceeded to diaper and dress her. Daisy kicked her legs, but didn't smile at the nanny or try to make eye contact.

"She waited an hour to change her after her nap?" Violet's forehead was furrowed. "It's not a crime, but it's certainly not what I expect from the person I pay to care for my child." In real-time, Daisy was starting to whimper and pull at Violet's shirt.

"Why don't you feed her while I scan the rest? If there's anything interesting, I'll let you know."

As far as Jake was concerned, they'd seen enough to fire Carrie. What he saw ten minutes later, however, made him wonder if they needed to do even more than that. "Violet?" he called up the stairs. "I think you'll want to see this."

*

Violet draped a blanket over the baby, who was still nursing, and returned to the living room. She found Jake literally sitting on the edge of his seat.

"Are you ready?" he asked her.

"What is it? She didn't hurt Daisy, did she?" The baby squirmed, feeling her tension. She forced a breath deep into her lungs, trying to relax so her milk wouldn't dry up.

"No." Jake reached over and squeezed her hand, then let it go and pressed "enter" on the keyboard.

The screen showed Carrie walking into the living room carrying Daisy. She set her down, much too roughly in Violet's opinion, on the play mat, then hurried into the foyer. After checking through the peephole, she opened the front door. A tall man entered and slapped Carrie across the face, hard enough to make her lose her balance and hit the wall.

Violet gasped and recoiled as though he had slapped *her*. As she watched, afraid of what she would see but unable to look away, Carrie tried to cover both her head and her upper body with her arms. The man appeared to be yelling, and his contorted face was inches away from hers.

"I believed her story about walking into a door! I was afraid she'd try to sue me. How could I be so naïve?"

Jake pressed a key and the computer's desktop appeared. "What's happening to that girl isn't something that happens in your world." His voice was soft.

"No, and I intend to keep it that way." Daisy stopped sucking and seemed content, so she slipped her out from under her shirt and pulled her clothes together before dropping the blanket.

"Here." She stood and dropped the baby into Jake's lap, the first time she'd done so willingly. "I'm going to call the agency. Maybe they can reach Carrie before she comes back here. The head of the agency should be the one to tell her she's fired."

"You don't think that maybe we should . . . help her in some way?"

She turned back to Jake with a sigh. "I may have been naïve about Carrie's injury, but as a reporter, I'm very much aware of the problem of abuse. You can't help someone who isn't ready to be helped, and my own life is much too complicated right now to worry about hers. We're just lucky Daisy wasn't hurt."

When he didn't reply and continued to make funny faces at Daisy, who was laughing from her belly, she went to the kitchen to make her call. Whatever Mr. Do-gooder thought, her child was her only concern, not the nanny.

Jake and Daisy weren't in the living room when she got off the phone. She felt a momentary jolt of fear, until she heard him singing upstairs. She went up to the nursery where she was startled to find Jake, naked from the waist up, changing a very odorous and messy diaper. He was singing "Bicycle Built for Two," which of course prominently featured his daughter's name and made her smile.

"Is there a story to go along with what I'm seeing?" she asked when he turned his head and saw her in the doorway. His scattering of chest hair was blonde against his golden tan, and she could see now that although he was thinner, he was rock-hard solid. If that's what yoga did for a man, classes should be mandatory.

"I forgot she just ate, and got carried away with the playing and bouncing. That's why I'm no longer wearing a shirt. Then I realized we had an even bigger mess."

"Would you like me to take over?"

He wrapped the soiled diaper and baby wipes up neatly and shot them into the disposal, never taking his left hand or his eyes off Daisy. Violet was impressed. Even Seth, an experienced father, handled diapers with the trepidation of someone cleaning up nuclear waste. And Richard turned puce if there was even talk of the baby needing a change.

"Mission accomplished."

When he lifted the baby, who was wearing only the diaper, against his chest, Violet's knees got weak. She felt a surge of desire to run her hands across his chest, to feel her own naked skin pressed against his.

"Is something wrong? Did I put the diaper on backwards?"

"No, of course not." She forced herself to look into his eyes instead of at his naked chest, and to focus on her crisis. "But I have a problem. The woman from the agency called Carrie and fired her, and they're going to send someone to pick up her things. But there won't be anyone available for me to interview until Monday at the earliest."

"You don't have anyone else to take care of Daisy? You don't have family here, or friends?"

She shook her head. "My mother and step-father live in Connecticut, my best friend lives in Wickham, and I don't know anyone in Boston who can just take off from work to babysit for me. I'll have to tell the station I need to stay home the rest of the week." Because she'd taken maternity leave so soon after being hired, Violet hated to take time off without notice. The young woman who filled in for her, the weekend anchor, was hungry to take her place — Violet knew because she'd been there.

Daisy yawned, totally unconcerned by her mother's problem.

"I can do it. All I ask in return is that you let me wash my shirt so I don't have to leave here like this today."

"You can . . ."

"Take care of Daisy while you're at work. Don't you think I can do it?"

He'd shown he was capable, and Daisy certainly liked him. Right now she was falling asleep in his arms. But she didn't want him to stay overnight in Carrie's room, even if it meant she got less sleep.

"We'll take shifts, and I'll leave as soon as you get home from work," he continued before she could object. "I'll even give up my Saturday visit this week. You'll hardly see me at all."

It wasn't like she had a lot of other options. "We can try it. I should have a replacement for Carrie early next week."

She couldn't believe she was allowing this. A week ago she'd been hoping to banish Jake from their lives completely; now she'd be happy if she could keep him from moving in.

*

"I have to call the doctor," Violet blurted as she opened the door for Jake at noon on Thursday. Daisy had slept late, then fussed and refused to nurse after Violet snatched her from her crib in a panic. "Either she's sick, or there's something wrong with my milk. Although when I pumped for tonight's bottle I seemed to have plenty."

She realized she was babbling about her breasts to Jake and flushed to the tips of her ears. Although she wanted to discourage any desire he might still have for her, and surely she'd just done that?

"Did I miss the big news while I was out of the country?"

"What are you talking about?"

"Unless they discovered a cure for the common cold, there's no point calling her doctor. See how she's rubbing her nose? You said you were afraid she'd catch Carrie's cold, and she has."

He dropped his knapsack and placed a palm against Daisy's forehead, very close to Violet's right breast. Which — along with the left one — felt enormously prominent, either because they were engorged with milk or because of her jabbering about them.

After what seemed like a very long time, he removed his hand. "She doesn't have a fever, so I think we can handle this ourselves for now."

Violet had followed the recommendations in her baby care book and purchased a thermometer, bulb syringe, and cool-mist vaporizer. She just hadn't imagined using any of them. "I won't go to work today."

He laughed. "She'll be sick for a week or more, and get up to a dozen colds a year. Can you miss that much work?"

"She won't have a cold every month. This isn't some Third World country!" This time the man was flat-out wrong, and she'd be happy to prove it.

"Go ahead, check your book." He tipped his head in the direction of the baby care manual on the coffee table, and then took the baby from her. Using the soft cloth diaper Violet had draped over her shoulder, he gently wiped the baby's nose. Even so, she didn't like it and complained with a weak cry that wrenched her mother's heart.

Verifying Jake's facts didn't seem all that important at the moment. "I'll go, but I'm coming home between broadcasts to check on her and see if she'll nurse."

"Whatever makes you feel better. But the bottle will probably work better for her. The smaller nipple won't block her breathing."

There had been far too much discussion of Violet's breasts for her comfort. "I'm going to get ready for work, if you can manage with Daisy for a while."

He just grinned in response.

By the time Violet got home that night, he'd set up the vaporizer and the nursery was full of cool mist. He showed her how to use the syringe to clear the baby's nose before she ate. Daisy didn't seem much worse than she had that morning, but she woke up during the night and didn't go back to sleep until Violet had sung to her, rocked her, and walked the floor for over two hours.

The next day, Friday, was more of the same. Jake insisted Violet take a nap before she went to work, but she still felt rocky when she got home at midnight. She wasn't sure if she was relieved she wouldn't have to go back to work until Monday afternoon, or terrified at the prospect of spending the next two days tending to a sick and miserable child all by herself.

She found Jake in the living room. Daisy was on his lap, frowning at the television.

"Don't you think she's a little young for late-night movies?"

"Hey, it got her to stop crying."

They exchanged a weak smile.

"She didn't eat much," he said. "I think if we suction her nose first, she might want to nurse. She needs the comfort as much as the nourishment."

"I'll change out of these clothes and meet you in the nursery."

As she removed her skirt and blazer and hung them in her closet, replacing them with pajama pants and her short robe, she could hear Jake in the next room, talking and singing to Daisy. The baby's sudden angry cry told her he'd done the nasal suctioning, and the thought of it made her wince. She hadn't been able to do it without getting snot all over Daisy's face, and she wasn't sure the baby had been able to breathe any better when she was done.

The nursery was lit only by the pale glow of Daisy's night-light. Violet sat in the glider and slid the baby inside her robe without worrying about Jake watching, for once. She was too darn tired to even care, and assumed he felt the same.

"You can go," she told him. "We'll be fine." Daisy latched on to the nipple right away, and, despite the snuffling and wheezy sounds she was making, soon was sucking steadily. Violet closed her eyes and felt herself drifting away.

"I'm not leaving tonight."

Her eyes flew open. "But . . ."

"You need a good night's sleep. No arguing."

Chapter Six

It only took Jake a few seconds to remember where he was when he woke up, a skill he'd honed over many years of waking up in strange places. He was on Violet's sofa with a stiff throw pillow under his head and a knitted afghan covering him. Sunlight poured through the sheer window curtains, and he heard Violet's voice over the baby monitor as she talked to Daisy.

"Damn!" He rubbed the sleep out of his eyes and bounded up the stairs to the nursery. "I was going to get up with her so you could sleep in," he said when he reached the open door to Daisy's room.

Violet was standing over the baby at the changing table, snapping up her onesie. She turned to him, smiling. "Daisy had other plans."

Her hair was disheveled, and the robe she'd been wearing when he guided her to bed last night was belted snugly at her slender waist. Although he knew the studio had provided her with a personal trainer to help her regain her figure after Daisy was born, she'd made the kind of progress that required self-discipline and determination — traits Jake believed they had in common. He just wished she didn't also have that annoying hardheadedness.

Daisy sneezed, sending snot flying into the air. Violet calmly grabbed a cloth diaper and cleaned off her face. The baby squirmed but didn't cry.

"I don't know why I didn't hear the baby monitor," he said.

"It isn't instinctual for you yet." She picked Daisy up and took a step toward him, still smiling. Her words had stung him, although he knew she hadn't meant them to. "Her cold seems better today."

"Great." That meant she wouldn't need him to stay, which was good. He had plenty of things he needed to do this weekend, although he couldn't remember exactly what they were at the moment.

"Would you take her for a minute while I get dressed? She already ate."

As they made the exchange, he saw the outline of her breasts through the cotton robe, and remembered the previous night. Violet had fallen asleep holding Daisy in the glider, and when he took the baby from her arms he'd had to pull her robe over her exposed breast. He had to admit he hadn't done it as quickly as he should have. Now he was experiencing the same physical reaction he had then, and grabbed a blanket from the crib to cover him and the baby.

"It's cool downstairs, I accidentally left a window open," he explained.

She just stared at him, biting her lip, and he remembered the first time he'd seen her on television at his Uncle Matt's — he'd thought she was the typical female talking head, coiffed and made-up and reciting the news in an unaccented, well-modulated voice. Not his type at all. But he'd felt compelled to keep watching, and discovered she wasn't as blandly perfect as he'd first thought. A wisp of her dark hair was out of place, and a shadow of grief crossed her face as she reported on a local tragedy with a slight quaver in her voice.

"Jake, I want you to know I appreciate all you've done for us this week. I couldn't have managed without you." Her brilliant blue eyes shone with emotion.

No, she was not an automaton. She was warm, caring, and vulnerable. He'd never seen anything more beautiful than this woman and her child. *His* child. Violet had been hurt and neglected by her own father, and he understood now why she'd kept her pregnancy a secret from him. If you don't care about someone, you can't be hurt. Those bright eyes belonged to someone who was starting to care.

"You'd have managed just fine without me," he told her, his voice gruff. "You're a terrific mother."

She sighed. "Being a single mother is harder than I expected."

"Well, you won't be one for much longer." He shifted Daisy to his shoulder, where she let out a moist burp.

Violet seemed confused for a moment. "Umm, about that . . ."

"Listen, I have to be somewhere, so why don't you shower and get dressed before I go?" He didn't want to hang around and talk about Richard the Clown and their marriage plans. "I'll put Daisy on her play mat and make you some breakfast."

The light seemed to go out of her eyes. "Sure. But don't worry about breakfast, I don't want to hold you up."

*

Violet showered and dressed at top speed, as eager to be rid of Jake as he was to leave. She'd been so relieved to have help with Daisy that she'd let down her guard, forgotten she had to be careful not to encourage Jake to get overly involved in Daisy's life — and hers. She'd been on the verge of telling him the truth about her relationship with Richard, when he'd given her a blunt reminder of her reason for wanting to keep him away. Because, of course, he'd always want to *be* somewhere else. Just like today. Last night he was tender and caring, but today he had something more *important* to do than spend time with his baby, or with her.

There was a mug of coffee waiting when she walked into the kitchen with no makeup and her hair still wet. Jake was bouncing a fussy Daisy in his arms, and there was the furrow of a frown on his forehead. He turned his warm amber gaze on her, and she felt her heart flip. When, exactly, had she relinquished control of her internal organs? Jake was getting to her, and it had to stop. Now.

"I thought you said you just fed her." There was something vaguely accusing in his tone, and suddenly he wasn't as attractive as he'd been a moment ago.

"I did."

"Well, she's hungry again."

"Maybe she's just crying because her nose is stuffed up, did you consider that?" She reached for Daisy, and grabbed her from Jake so roughly she cried even louder. "Shh, shh, it's alright. Mommy will suction your nose."

"I just *did* that. Why don't you try feeding her again?" He hoisted his backpack, which had been hanging from one of the kitchen chairs. "I have to check in with my brother, but you can call me on my cell if you need to."

He was out of there so fast he never even heard her retort. Not that he could have, over the sound of Daisy wailing. "Believe me, I won't *need* you," she said to the closed door.

As soon as she settled in the rocker and lifted her shirt, Daisy clamped on to her nipple and started sucking. "Well, I guess you *were* hungry." What disturbed her more than Jake being right was that the baby had nursed just as long as usual at the earlier feeding. She'd been restless, turning away frequently, but Violet had blamed it on her cold.

After only a minute or so of frantic sucking, Daisy spit out the nipple and began to howl again, tears streaming down her red, angry face. Violet realized then that she hadn't felt her milk let down. Maybe because of the stress of the past week, or the supplemental bottles they'd given Daisy, it appeared that her milk had dried up. But it didn't matter why, she thought, what mattered was that she could no longer feed her child, the most elemental task of motherhood. Her body really *had* betrayed her.

Tears sliding down her face as well, she reached for the phone on the table beside her and pressed "1" on speed dial. Her call was answered on the second ring, by the only person whose voice she wanted to hear at that moment.

"Mom? Can you come to Boston — today?"

*

When Jake arrived at his brother's penthouse, he wasn't sure he should use his key, or even if it would work. Pamela had probably had the locks changed and switched the décor to Country Cottage by now.

"Hello?" he called, his voice lost in the vast space.

"Back here." Jamie was in his home office, standing over a sheaf of blueprints on his architect's desk. "I wondered when the prodigal brother was going to show up."

"Sorry about that. I just had to . . ."

"Go. I know. It's what you do. What you've always done." His eyes were hard to read behind his stylish black-framed glasses, but Jake heard resignation in his voice, and acceptance. "Have you been in touch with Uncle Matt?"

Calling Uncle Matt had been at the top of his list, until Violet lost her nanny. "No, why?"

Jamie ran his hand through his hair, which was the same dark blonde color as Jake's but longer and curlier. "He fell on a job a couple days ago, got a concussion and broke his leg. He's going to be out on disability for six weeks, at least."

"Whew, that's going to be hard for him to take." His uncle bragged, with annoying frequency, that he hadn't missed a day of work since he was sixteen. "At least he has Darlene to help him." Or was it Darla? It was hard to keep track of Matt's women — a family trait.

His brother laughed. "*Donna* moved out a few months after you left for the last trip. She said he was impossible to live with. A nurse is going to check on him every few days, but otherwise he's on his own."

"I don't have any plans the rest of the weekend." Unless Violet called him, of course, but he was pretty sure that wasn't going to happen. He hadn't liked treating her so coldly, but felt it was necessary — for both their sakes. "I'll drive to Wickham to see how he's doing. But I came over to explain about what happened the other day."

The click-clack of high heels on the wooden floors told him he and Jamie weren't alone in the apartment after all.

"Jamie? Our appointment's in half an hour." Pamela was checking her watch as she entered the room. She appeared surprised to see Jake, although he knew she must have heard the two men talking before she came in. "Jake! How nice to see you again."

He nodded and forced his lips into something she might consider a smile.

Jamie rolled up the blueprints. "We're going to pick out new carpeting for the master bedroom." Jake expected eye-rolling, but his brother seemed enthusiastic. "But stick around and we'll all have dinner together. You have something important to tell us, right?"

Jake shrugged. "It can wait. I'd better stay at Uncle Matt's tonight."

*

"Where have you been, boy? Holed up with some woman, no doubt." His strong and powerful uncle crammed into a wheelchair, with his leg in a mammoth cast extended straight in front of him, was an arresting sight.

"*Two* women. But how was I supposed to know you would fall off a roof?"

"Ha! I could believe your brother was with two women, but not you. And I didn't fall off a roof. As you well know, I have the balance of a mountain goat." Although he'd managed to open the door for Jake, Matt was having difficulty maneuvering the chair from the entryway back to the living room.

"Let me give you a hand." His uncle glared at him, so Jake backed away and waited for him to jockey the chair into the right angle to make it through the narrow doorway. Once he was back in the living room, which was uncharacteristically strewn with books, newspapers, and even clothes, he picked up the cable remote and began channel surfing, pointedly ignoring Jake.

"Uncle Matt? How did you get hurt?"

The big man curled his lip like a baby. Like Daisy had after he suctioned her nose, in fact. "I was watching my client walk back to her car. She has the most amazing ass I've ever seen, Jake, I swear. And I . . . " The rest was garbled.

"I'm sorry?"

"I stepped into the basement we'd just excavated, like some stupid cartoon character!"

Jake's first impulse was to laugh at the image, but he was smart enough to stifle it. "I guess you made quite an impression on your client."

"She drove away in her Mercedes before anyone knew what happened. At least I'm thankful for that."

"Maybe you should be thankful your men hadn't poured the cement yet."

Matt's mouth fell open, and then he began to laugh. Jake joined in after a beat, and they kept it up in wave after wave until their eyes watered and his uncle started to cough.

"Didn't even occur to me," he wheezed.

"Let me get you something to drink. A beer? I'm spending the weekend, and I plan to knock back a few myself." Some American vices didn't seem so bad anymore.

Jake headed for the kitchen, but when his uncle got his breath back he tried to stop him. "I haven't had a chance to get things cleaned up. I didn't know you were coming."

"Just relax. I'm here to help." Except he hadn't expected his normally fastidious uncle's kitchen would look like a tornado had come through and emptied his cupboards and refrigerator. It was a good thing they didn't need glasses for their beer. He filled the sink with hot soapy water and dumped the crustiest dishes and pans in to soak.

"Did you have a falling out with Jamie?" Uncle Matt asked when he brought him his beer. "Because you can stay here while you finish work on your books."

Jake wasn't sure if the offer was for his benefit or Matt's. It was obvious his uncle was going to need some help, and Jake could work in Wickham and drive in to Boston when he needed. But there was his visitation with Daisy on Saturdays, which he'd already decided wasn't going to be enough.

He shook his head and stared at his beer bottle as if it had all the answers. *Just say it.* He took a deep breath. "Here's the thing, Uncle Matt. I've got a kid in Boston."

"Did you know I had a concussion? Because I just thought you said you had a *kid*, Jake." Matt's expression was two parts confusion and one part shock.

"You heard right. I have a baby girl named Daisy, and it's your fault."

His uncle killed the television from the remote and turned his wheelchair to face Jake straight on. "You've blamed a lot of things on me over the years, but I think you'll have a tough time making this charge stick."

"You introduced me to her mother, last year at about this time."

Just when Jake thought he was going to have to spell it out, Matt's face lit up with the pleasure of solving a riddle. "Violet Gallagher! I knew she had a baby, but I never thought . . ." He whistled, which made his old retriever, Rex, stagger in from the back porch and blink at them with rheumy eyes. "She's a real beauty, and a sweet girl, too. There was a time I considered asking her out myself. But how come you never told us about the baby?"

Jake slammed his beer down on the end table next to his chair. He might understand now why Violet had kept the baby a secret, but he hadn't forgiven her.

"I didn't know. I'm not proud of it, but what happened between us was meant to be a one-night stand. How could it be anything else? I was leaving for Russia the next day. So when she found out she was pregnant, she decided she could do it on her own. I had to figure it out for myself when I got home."

"No, no, no. This single-mother stuff is no good! Amanda,

your poor mother, struggled so much after my brother died. Then she married that creep Ellsworth, probably just so she wouldn't have to do it all alone." He rubbed his eyes with his fists, as though he wanted to erase the vile memories. "But you know now, Jake, so what are you going to do about it?"

Jake opened and closed his mouth. Leave it to Uncle Matt to ask the hard questions. "Now I'm going to . . . wash your dishes." He escaped to the kitchen, leaving Matt mumbling and swearing as he tried to follow in the uncooperative chair.

"Rex, get back to the porch before I run you over with this contraption!"

By the time his uncle made it to the kitchen, Jake was up to his elbows in soapy water. He was in hot water, it turned out, in more ways than one.

"Jake, I asked you a question." His uncle's voice was soft, in the ominous way he and Jamie knew was far more serious than if he bellowed at them.

"You think I should make an honest woman of her? When your own bedroom has a revolving door?"

Jake felt his uncle's piercing glare without turning around. "I never fathered a child."

He didn't dare remind his uncle, but he usually followed that statement with *as far as I know*. "I intend to be a father to my child, as much as I'm able to with my work and to the extent Violet allows. As for Violet, I can't force myself on her."

"You're sure she doesn't want you?"

"We spent one night together. We don't even know each other." To be honest, he felt like he knew her much better after last night. Taking care of their sick baby together felt more intimate than the act that had created her.

"When do men and women ever really know each other? Do you think your mother knew Ellsworth?"

Jake's fists clenched in the dishwater. Although his logic was skewed, damn Uncle Matt for making him think about George Ellsworth, the man who'd knocked his mother around, then abandoned her when her cancer was diagnosed. He would have as little say about who came into Violet's life as his dead father had had, and about an equal ability to protect her. Richard Rayburn might be with Violet right at this moment, attempting to insinuate himself into her life permanently. He supposed he should be grateful; the man seemed harmless enough. But he wasn't grateful, not at all. Violet — and Daisy — deserved better. There was only one way to ensure they got it, and that way was impossible. For several reasons.

"What are my wife and child supposed to do while I'm in Nairobi or Bhutan for months at a time? I have to make a living." He handed his uncle a dish towel.

Matt shook his head in apparent disgust and wheeled closer to the stack of washed dishes. "Your cameras work here in the States, don't they? Here in Massachusetts?"

The very idea of *staying home* made Jake's throat start to close up.

"I have a contract with my publisher. A legal document, Uncle Matt."

The other man sighed. "Jake, I raised you to do the right thing. The right thing and the legal thing are not always the same."

He drained the sink and began to fill it again, wondering how his uncle had managed to use so many dishes in the short time since his accident. In the silence that followed, he heard loud and clear the things his uncle wasn't saying, the things he never said.

When his mother died, George Ellsworth, the man who had left her to die with only her young sons to care for her, became their legal guardian. But Matt, their father's much younger brother and a complete stranger to them, had come to their rescue. It hadn't taken much for him to convince Ellsworth to step aside, once the man knew there was no inheritance to leech. Although it was unremarkable to him at the time, Jake often reflected these days on the most significant aspect of the story. Matt was only twenty-one years old at the time. Whatever his plans might have been, they were abandoned to raise and support two emotionally scarred hellions who never showed, as Matt himself might have said but didn't, a lick of gratitude. There was no revolving door on Matt's bedroom in those days, and now, although Jake supposed it wasn't too late, he had no wife or children of his own. He had no idea if his uncle had ever wanted those things. Until now.

"You have a child, Jake, and she has a beautiful, sweet, smart mother. You've got what? Three months before you have to figure out what to do about your job? Get out of here and go after your family!"

*

By Sunday afternoon, Violet had accepted that she was finished with breastfeeding. According to what she read on the Internet, it was possible to restore her milk, but it was more work than she felt herself capable of at the moment. Daisy had no nanny, and her mother had to leave in a couple of hours.

"I'm sorry, Violet, but the cruise to the Greek Isles won't wait for me," Sandra poured a cup of the special blend tea she'd brought with her into one of Violet's best antique China cups. It was a scene straight out of her childhood — her mother bustling about the kitchen in a worn pair of jeans and a man's white shirt, while Violet sat at the table, having a snack and describing her day. The only difference was Daisy's presence, her soft breathing coming through the baby monitor on the counter while she napped upstairs.

Her mother set the cup in front of her and Violet inhaled the herb-scented steam. "Oh, Mom, I understand."

Although her mother still worked as an elementary school principal, her stepfather was retired. Sandra's time off was sacred, and usually spent traveling. Sometimes Violet considered the irony of having her mother out of the country a third of the year. At the age of twelve she'd envisioned herself becoming a journalist who traveled the world, following the hottest stories. But in the end, she couldn't abandon her mother the way Monty had. Now she felt like her mother was abandoning *her*.

"If you don't find a nanny tomorrow, you can ask Jake to come back and help, right?"

Violet sighed. "He ran out of here so fast yesterday, you'd have thought the house was on fire."

"Why wouldn't he?" Sandra's lips tightened and she scrubbed the sink harder. "You've been trying to run him off since he got here."

"Because his running off is inevitable. Might as well get it over with."

Sandra poured her own cup of tea and sat across from Violet at the glass-tiled table. "You seem to know an awful lot about a man you spent one night with. I've been with David for fifteen years, and I still can't predict what he might do."

Violet hated it when her mother went into teacher mode. "He's an 'artist.' He travels. He's just like . . ."

"Your father?" Sandra smiled and blew on her tea. "I very much doubt it. But I haven't met the man."

Violet hoped to keep it that way. "You remember Richard Rayburn, don't you? I let Jake think I'm seeing him." She'd let Jake think she was *marrying* him, but she didn't tell her mother that. "He's in love with me, and I'm hoping I might feel the same if I give him a chance. He's a good man. In fact, he reminds me of David."

Sandra slammed her cup down on its saucer so hard the delicate handle broke off in her hand. She and Violet stared at it, momentarily stunned. Then they both began to laugh. Her mother was the first to stop. "Oh, Violet, you're *hoping* you'll love him? I have nothing against Richard, but that isn't how these things work." She picked up the cup handle and surveyed the damage.

"I'll take this home with me. David has some wonderful glue, I'm sure he can fix it."

"Mom, you always told me not to save the good stuff for a special occasion. So you broke one of Grandma Foster's cups. What are there, about seventeen more?"

"But . . ." The doorbell interrupted her mother's protestation.

Violet sighed. "It's probably Richard. He's taken to popping in unexpectedly."

Her mother's voice followed her out of the kitchen. "I have to say, you don't sound very happy to see the man you're *hoping* to fall in love with."

Score one for Mom.

She forced a smile and flung open the door, only to find herself face to face with Jake, who responded with a big grin of his own. "Oh." She crossed her arms over her chest. "I wasn't expecting you." Just so he'd know her pleasant expression hadn't been meant for him.

"Can I come in? I have a proposal for you."

"A proposal?" Her mother said from behind her. "How delightful! This must be Jake, I can see Daisy's bone structure in his face."

Violet didn't bother turning around. "Jake, this is my mother, Sandra Gallagher."

He stepped inside and reached for her mother's hand. "Sandra? As in the first hit song by the Ultimates?"

"Yes, it's *Sultry Sandra*, in the flesh," Violet said. When she was a teenager, the existence of a famous album cover graced with a picture of her mother wearing only an oversized man's white shirt had been her greatest embarrassment in life.

"That was a long time ago," Sandra said. "I was just a girl."

Violet watched as Jake scanned her mother from top to bottom the way men do when they meet an attractive woman, taking in the fact that she was once again dressed in a man's shirt. "You've only improved with age, and now I see where Violet gets her beauty. I knew it wasn't from Monty McCall."

"Oh, Monty was handsome as a young man. Before he . . ." She was interrupted by a cry from Daisy, heard in stereo from upstairs and the monitor in the kitchen. "I'll take up a bottle and feed her. Violet, you take this charming man into the living room and find out what it is he's proposing."

Chapter Seven

"Why is your mother giving Daisy a bottle?" Jake took a seat on the couch.

"My milk has . . . dried up. I think what happened with Carrie, and Daisy being sick, was just too stressful. I wasn't planning to nurse much longer anyway, so it's not a big deal."

She could feel her face flush crimson. Although she'd prefer not to tell him, he was around enough that he'd have to find out. She only hoped this would be the *last* conversation they'd have about her breasts.

To her surprise, he began to fold the tiny baby garments in a laundry basket on the coffee table. Violet wondered what he was thinking. She knew his opinions about mothering the natural way, but it wasn't her fault her milk had dried up. Or was it? She'd cried for half an hour last night, and felt her eyes welling up again. Her emotions hadn't been this unstable since the days immediately following Daisy's birth, when she had often wept for no reason at all.

"Too bad," he finally said. "I hear it's a wonderful experience. But I'm sure you'll have another opportunity someday."

Would she? She bent her head, embarrassed by her tears. Her life plan had never gone beyond one child, and, since a husband hadn't yet materialized, a second child was hardly an option. Which reminded her of what he'd said on her doorstep.

"You have a proposal for me?"

"Something that will benefit us both, and Daisy most of all."

He paused to concentrate on folding a fitted crib sheet, making sure the corners were tucked inside each other, while her mind raced with possibilities. Could his proposal possibly be marriage? For Daisy's sake, if no other reason?

"I need a place to live," he continued, "and you need a nanny."

Not marriage, then — of course not. But why did he need a place to live? She had suspected he was living with a woman. Had she thrown him out?

"I usually stay with my brother while I work on my books, but he has a woman living with him now, and three's a crowd." He grinned at her.

He'd been living with his brother? That didn't mean he hadn't spent a night or two elsewhere, she reminded herself.

"I'm interviewing nannies tomorrow." She'd been dreading the task. Carrie had seemed entirely suitable at her interview, and Violet didn't trust her instincts now.

"If I stay here for three months until I have to leave for South America to shoot the next book, you'll have more time to find the right person. Meanwhile, I can get my work done after Daisy goes to bed."

It seemed like an ideal, if temporary, solution. Daisy loved Jake, and Violet wouldn't have to let another stranger into her home. However, she'd have to let *Jake* into her home. Tempting, handsome Jake, who was staring at her with those deep amber eyes, waiting for her answer.

"You really need someplace to stay?"

He grinned at her. "You wouldn't have to worry. It would be a business arrangement, more or less."

Violet wasn't sure if she wanted it to be more — or less. She swallowed, hard. "Can you move in tonight?"

*

Her mother came down the stairs with Daisy in her arms just as the door closed behind Jake. "You let him leave without saying goodbye? He didn't even see Daisy."

"He had an appointment with his agent. And he's going to see Daisy every day for the next three months. Jake's going to be her new nanny."

Sandra put Daisy under the play gym. "Shame on you, Violet. He's her *daddy*, not her nanny. But I'm glad that problem is solved." She joined her mother on the floor. "Only short-term. Then he'll be gone again for a year."

"Maybe not."

Violet laughed. "I don't know how you can still be such a romantic, after what happened with Monty."

"I've never spent a minute regretting my marriage to Monty, and not just because you and Seth came out of it." Sandra stopped shaking a rattle at Daisy and looked straight at Violet. "I loved Monty. He was a good man."

She raised her eyebrows at her mother, who smiled and held up a slender, manicured hand.

"I know, that's not what you saw. Unfortunately for us, it was the music he loved the most, and the rock-star lifestyle was lethal for him. He was an addict, Violet. He tried a couple times to get clean, but he was surrounded by people doing the thing he was trying to stop."

Violet checked her watch. "I hate to say it, but it's time to call you a cab." She knew addiction was a disease, but she wasn't ready to forgive her father for his neglect.

Her mother kissed Daisy and rose gracefully from the floor. "In any case, your Jake is *not* Monty McCall. Give him a chance to show you who he is."

Violet picked up the baby and stood beside her mother. "I'm not sure who he is, but I know who he's not — *my* Jake."

*

After Jake promised Violet he'd move into the nanny's room later that evening, he went to see Millie Winston, his agent, for a special Sunday meeting at her apartment. She'd scheduled a show of his work at a Boston gallery later in the summer, and wanted to go over the slides with him.

After viewing some of his work from Russia, she sipped her tea and smiled at him. Millie always smiled, but he'd learned to tell the difference between the polite smiles and the real ones. This one was genuine.

"We've been giving you a rugged-adventurer image, Jake, but maybe we should be emphasizing your paternal side."

"Paternal side?" Could Millie know about Daisy? He'd only told his uncle, and Matt didn't exactly travel in the Boston art circles.

She pointed to one of the slides. "Maybe not paternal, exactly, but softer. You have a real affinity for mothers and children. Some of your best pictures have a definite Madonna quality."

He laughed with relief. Coming out as a father was something he'd have to do eventually, but he still had some time. When he examined the picture Millie was talking about, his mind flashed to a photograph his mother had proudly displayed in their living room, the only studio portrait the family had ever had taken. In it, Jamie and Jake were enfolded in their beaming mother's arms. The arrangement of the Russian mother and her two sons echoed it exactly.

"My mother died when I was a young teenager," he told Millie. "I think that's why I'm drawn to mothers and their children. The photographs are my attempt to show the special bond they have." His thoughts were a revelation. Was that really what he'd been doing? He'd only known he'd seen beauty in the women, no matter what their physical appearance.

Millie nodded silently, lost in her own thoughts. Was crusty old Millie thinking about her own mother? Did she have a sentimental side he'd never seen?

"Jake, I think we should work this angle," she said.

So much for sentiment.

It was seven o'clock by the time Jake and Millie finished, and he headed to his brother's, hoping the apartment would be empty. It was. If he hurried, he could pack a duffel bag with most of his belongings and get back to Violet's before his brother — or God forbid, Pamela — showed up. It wasn't that he didn't plan to talk to Jamie. He just wasn't sure he wanted to hear what Jamie had to say to him right now. Any more advice and he might just have to pack his bag and take an unscheduled trip.

The sound of the elevator door opening at the penthouse floor and footsteps on the wooden floor told him he was trapped. He hoisted his bag over his shoulder, hoping to at least keep the lecture brief, and stepped out into the hallway.

"I'm sorry I didn't return your calls," he said to his brother. "I've been busy."

Jamie laughed and tossed his mail onto the credenza. "So I hear."

"You talked to Uncle Matt?"

He nodded, and furrows formed between his dark eyebrows. "I'm really sorry about the other day. All those things we said about Violet..."

"You didn't know."

Jamie immediately brightened. For the brothers, the brief conversation meant *all is forgiven, let's move on.*

"So, wow, I'm an uncle! This calls for a celebration. Uncle Matt also told me you're no longer on the wagon, so let's head down the street for a drink."

"Will Pamela be joining us?" Jake left his bag next to the credenza and followed his brother onto the elevator.

"No, she's meeting with clients. I know you don't like her, Jake, and it's okay. Maybe I won't like your Violet, either."

"She's not *my* Violet." Although he couldn't imagine why anyone would not like Violet.

"No? Where were you headed with that bag?"

Their eyes met in the mirrored door, and Jake knew by his brother's grin he had his number. He shrugged. "I didn't plan this, I didn't expect it, and I sure as hell don't know what I'm doing about it. Other than moving in to be my daughter's unpaid nanny for the next three months."

Ten minutes later they were settled in a booth in the bar down the street, clinking their bottles of Sam Adams together.

"So, she's pretty cute, huh?"

"You've seen her on television."

Jamie laughed. "I meant the baby. Hopefully she takes after her mother."

"A little bit. She also looks like me, and you, and both our parents. It's amazing, Jamie. What's even more amazing is how I feel about her. I want to give her the world. I'd do anything to keep her safe and make her happy."

Jamie scraped at the label on his beer bottle. "I'm sure Dad felt that way about us, too. But even if he'd been around, he wouldn't have been able to do those things. Nobody can."

"Uncle Matt thinks I should marry Violet, just because she's the mother of my child. But even if we fell in love, it wouldn't be fair to her. I have to travel."

Jamie leaned back and stared at his brother for a long time. "When you were a kid, and our lives were so grim, you always had your nose stuck in a book about some faraway place. You picked up a camera, discovered you were good, and got other people to pay for you to go to those places. You've been escaping all your life, or trying to."

Jake had to laugh. Matt and Jamie were on the same side of the commitment scale he was, but suddenly they were acting like he was out there all alone. "What's your point?"

"There's a saying — 'everywhere you go, there you are.' Maybe the thing you're trying to escape from is inside of you."

The Zen master had said similar things, although not with the bluntness of his brother. "Jamie Macintyre, philosopher. Maybe traveling and taking pictures is just what I do, the way you design buildings and Uncle Matt builds them."

Jamie raised his hand to flag down the waitress. "Ignore me, little brother. You've got plenty of time to figure it out. But we need to decide what we're going to do about Uncle Matt. He won't admit it, but he needs help."

*

After he and Jamie worked out an arrangement for checking on their uncle until they could hire someone to help, Jake retrieved his bag and headed for his new home. He had a key, but Violet had told him she'd feel more comfortable if he rang the bell before he used it. When she didn't come to the door within a minute or two, he let himself in.

"Violet?" He'd told her he would respect her privacy, but if Rayburn's car had been parked out front he would have barged right in.

"Back here."

He followed her voice out to the deck off the kitchen, where she was stretched out on a chaise, holding Daisy against her chest.

"Enjoying the sunset?"

When the baby heard his voice, she raised her head and smiled at him. After a moment it crashed back down, slamming against her mother's chin. "Ouch!" Violet laughed. "Everything was lovely until just now."

"I'd forgotten how beautiful a Massachusetts sunset can be." The day had been cloudy, and now the cloud layers were reflecting shades of pink, purple and red. He unzipped his duffle bag and pulled out a camera, made a few adjustments, and began to snap off shots.

After a few minutes he stopped, and saw Daisy smile at him again, this time with her head against Violet's chest but held securely in place by her hand. When Violet also smiled in his direction, he lifted the camera, focused in tightly, and clicked the shutter.

Violet's hand flew to her hair. "Will you be doing this a lot?"

He laughed. "Violet, I saw your face on a billboard yesterday. Your nose was ten feet long. You're in front of cameras every day."

"Yes, *after* people do my hair and make-up and even tell me what to wear. Candid shots are different. Scarier."

"If you like the picture I just took, will you let me take more? They won't be candids, but they won't be studio shots, either."

Daisy was falling asleep, and Violet swung her legs around so she could get out of the chair. Beautiful long legs with well-defined muscles. "Well, I haven't had professional pictures done of Daisy since she was a few weeks old."

He returned the camera to the bag. "I'll take pictures of Daisy, but only if you let me take some of the two of you together." As he'd discovered during his conversation with Millie, there was something magical in the mother-child connection for him. What better models to use to mine that theme?

She smiled. "If I like your work."

*

Violet had always enjoyed Daisy's early-morning feeding; the two of them nestled together in her bed as the sun rose and the rest of the world began to stir, beginning with the robins and house finches outside her window. She had not enjoyed handing her over to Carrie afterwards and going back to sleep, but it was the only way she could make it through the 11:00 p.m. news and not drive her car off the road at midnight.

When she woke up on Monday morning to the sound of birds singing and realized Jake must have gotten Daisy up for her feeding, she felt a sharp twinge of disappointment. It had been bad enough to hear Daisy begin to fuss the last few mornings and not feel the familiar pressure of the milk in her breasts, but at least she'd been able to continue her morning ritual while substituting a bottle of formula.

She was still tying the sash of her robe when she walked into the nursery, where Jake was giving Daisy her bottle while standing next to the open window. Her first thought was that his method would upset Daisy, disrupting her routine and sense of security.

But the baby's expression was one of rapture as she gazed into his face; it was the same way she looked at Violet while she nursed.

"Do you hear that? A cardinal is calling to his mate. We'll set up a bird feeder, and we'll get lots of feathered visitors. But today, we'll take a trip to the park and take some pictures. Not a lot of wildlife there, just squirrels and pigeons."

"And who will feed the birds after you're gone?"

If he was surprised Violet was standing behind him, he didn't show it. "If it's too difficult for you to throw a cup of seeds in the feeder every morning, I won't do it. I was planning to ask you first." His grin implied he thought she was being unreasonable and grumpy, and it infuriated her. Probably because it was true.

It wasn't the idea of stocking bird seed that upset her; it was his mention of an outing to the park, something Carrie had done with Daisy almost every day. Carrie did it so she and the baby could get some fresh air and see other people, or at least that's what Violet had thought at the time. Now she wasn't sure *what* the nanny had been up to. But Jake called it "a trip," which made her feel like he was seducing Daisy into his world.

Half her child's DNA had come from him, after all, and soon it might be her daughter who was abandoning her for months at a time. Right now nine hours apart was too long. Realizing how foolish it would sound if she said that to Jake, she forced herself to focus on the original issue that had brought her flying into the nursery without even pulling a brush through her hair first.

"She's getting formula now, so it isn't strictly necessary, but I'd prefer to give Daisy her morning feeding. It's a routine we're both used to."

"It just seemed more efficient for me to do it. Then when you get up, you're up for the day. The quality of your sleep will be better." Daisy had finished the bottle, and he pulled it from her mouth with a pop as the suction broke. When she saw her mother, she smiled and strained her body toward her, waving her plump arms and legs.

"I'm a mother. My sleep is not supposed to be high quality." Even as she took the baby from Jake, she noticed the fullness of her bladder. She watched him sip from a cup of coffee, and felt herself craving it with all her being. Daisy's sudden frown of concentration told her she'd soon need a diaper change.

"Hello, sweetheart," she crooned to her smiling baby. "Umm, Jake, I need to do some things. Would you mind taking her back for just a couple minutes?"

He laughed, wrinkling his nose as the odor hit him. "Sure, you'll do the feeding, and I'll do the dirty work. Get yourself a cup of coffee after you do those . . . things, and we'll meet you downstairs."

In the bathroom, Violet bent over and ran a brush through her hair, trying to instill some life into it. She rubbed tinted moisturizer on her face, but forced herself to stop short of mascara. Having Jake here is no different from having a nanny, she told herself, tossing the tube back in the drawer. Except it sure felt different.

She threw on some exercise clothes and got to the kitchen before Jake did. It was nice to have hot coffee waiting for her, she had to admit, a luxury that had not been provided by the nanny, who was a tea drinker. As she reached for the sugar, she realized the bowl was anchoring a photograph. She slid it out, and saw it was the picture Jake had taken the night before, of her and Daisy relaxing out on the deck, surrounded by the rosy glow of the sunset. It was so unlike her studio shots she hardly recognized herself. For one thing, her smile in this picture was genuine.

"You like it, right?" he asked from behind her. "So you'll pose for me?"

Although she knew what he meant, something about his use of the word "pose" made her blush to the roots of her hair. She was glad she still had her back to him, and took a deep breath in an attempt to regain her composure.

"I'd say you have a real talent for this photography stuff." The research she'd done after their night together last summer had revealed there were quite a lot of experts and book-buyers who agreed. "How can I turn down the opportunity to get the best for free?"

In truth, something about it made her uncomfortable, but it wasn't anything she could articulate. Jake seemed to *see* her through the lens of his camera, in a way she didn't usually allow.

She turned toward him, finally. He was holding Daisy against his chest, and she had a fistful of his shirt in her hand. His grin lit up his face but he didn't say anything.

"They *will* be free, right?"

He came out of his trance. "That depends on your framing choices, ma'am. And of course wallets are extra."

The phone rang, and she was still laughing when she picked up and said hello.

There was a brief silence on the other end, then Richard said, "You're in a good mood this morning. You must have found a new nanny."

"Oh, Richard!" For Jake's benefit, she sounded more enthusiastic than she felt. "I do have the nanny situation taken care of, yes. But I don't have time to explain it to you right now."

"Well, why don't you explain it to me on Saturday night, over dinner? Now that you have someone to stay with Daisy."

"Sounds wonderful, but I'll have to check with . . . the nanny first. Why don't I call you back?"

Jake agreed to stay with Daisy on Saturday night, on one condition. "We'll do a photo session on Saturday, whatever time works best for Daisy. And I'll need to leave here early on Sunday to go see my uncle in Wickham, so don't stay out all night with your boyfriend."

"Richard isn't . . . expecting me to stay overnight," she finished, narrowly avoiding a slip. "But it will be wonderful to go out on a real date. Thanks for helping out."

His only response was a scowl that made Daisy burst into tears.

Violet had no idea how she would continue to fend Richard off while also leading him on, but with Jake living in her house, she felt it was crucial to keep a buffer between them. Or, as Jake had referred to Richard, a *buffoon*.

*

After Violet left for a session with her personal trainer, Jake packed up the baby's supplies and wheeled her off to the park in her deluxe baby stroller. The expensive conveyance made him shake his head and wonder what the mothers in some of the villages he'd visited would make of it. They would probably think Daisy was royalty, bow down to her and bring her gifts of root vegetables and small game.

"Your mom says you're ready to try some rice cereal, little princess, but I think we'll draw the line at small game." He lifted the eager baby out of the stroller and settled in the shade on a bench where they could watch the activity around them.

When a young woman asked him a few minutes later if she could share the bench, he agreed. She pulled a book out of her purse, but he noticed she never turned the page. Instead of reading, she kept taking sidelong glances at him and Daisy. Probably noticed his lack of a wedding ring. He'd heard the presence of babies or dogs made a man more attractive to women, and smiled to himself. She was attractive, but he didn't need any more entanglements. After a couple quick glances of his own, however, he began to think there was something familiar about her.

Daisy jerked her arm and the teething ring she'd been gripping in her fist hit the ground near the stranger. The woman lunged for it, then held it out to Jake. "Sorry, Daisy," she said. "You can't have it back now. It's dirty."

Jake gripped the baby hard enough to make her whimper.

"How do you know my baby's name?" But he figured it out before she could answer. The bruises on her upper arm had obviously been made by the tight grip of a man's hand.

"You're Carrie!"

The former nanny seemed to shrink into the corner of the bench, but she made no move to leave. Her voice was so soft Jake had to strain to hear her.

"I came here on purpose hoping to talk to you. I knew I wouldn't get anywhere with Miss Gallagher."

"Well, you won't get anywhere with me, either. You were hired to care for her child, not bring your personal problems into her home."

"Your child, too. I know you're her daddy, and you seem like a good man. But all men aren't like you."

A memory of George Ellsworth hitting his mother with an open palm flashed into Jake's head. But whatever this young woman wanted, he didn't see how he could help her. "Yes, I'm Daisy's father. And she's getting sleepy and needs a nap, so you should make your point."

"I got involved with a bad man." She shuddered, and tears leaked from her eyes, one of which was still swollen and sporting a colorful bruise. "He beat me up real bad when he found out I got fired, and without a job I can't afford to leave him. He's talking about making me do things for money, things I can't do."

Jake was a sucker for a crying female. "Carrie, I can't give you your job back. You need to go to a shelter . . ."

She shook her head. "He'd find me. I need to go far away. The trouble is, I don't have any references to get another job."

Daisy was falling asleep on his shoulder, and he felt like a bad father. He knew he should get her home and in her crib before Violet returned from the gym. He stood and eased her into her stroller, then pulled a business card out of his wallet. Carrie didn't move, but her tears flowed faster.

"I would never have hurt your baby, she's the sweetest little thing. But he just wouldn't leave me alone to do my job."

He handed her the card. "I believe you. I'll try to help you, although you shouldn't count on it." An idea had just come to him, a live-in position out of town, caring for someone far less vulnerable than Daisy. But first he'd have to convince Uncle Matt he needed someone to help him. "Is there a number where I can call you? Your cell?"

Her good eye opened wide. "No! He checks it."

Jake sighed. "Okay, then you'll have to call me. Use my cell number and try to call tomorrow night." If Violet found out he was helping the woman, she'd be furious. He knew he was endangering his own position, but he'd vowed as a young boy that when he got to be a man he'd never let anyone hurt a woman the way Ellsworth had hurt his mother.

"If you ever feel like you're in real danger, call 911 or go to a shelter."

She nodded her head. He wanted to make her promise, but he knew there was no point.

Chapter Eight

"Go easy on the make-up," Jake said from outside Violet's bathroom door on Saturday. "Unlike your television station, I want to bring out your natural beauty."

She opened the door. "Are you saying you don't like how I look when I'm working?" She knew he didn't find her unattractive at home, because she often caught his appreciative glances as she was doing things with Daisy.

He grinned. "Violet, you're a beautiful woman. But there's more than one type of beauty."

"Are a little blush and some lipstick appropriate for the type of beauty you want?"

"Perfect. Most of the shoot will be in black-and-white anyway."

She closed the door and turned back to her mirror. Jake had originally suggested they do some "tasteful" shots with Violet and the baby both naked, or appearing to be, but she was so shocked he immediately backed down. Instead she was wearing white spandex shorts and a tank top to reveal her "long and slender" arms and legs, and the baby would wear a diaper.

Her sessions with the trainer had gotten rid of most of the pregnancy weight, and the spandex hid what was left. Best of all, her face was no longer puffy and tired-looking. She'd relented and allowed Jake to do the morning feeding, and she was now as energetic as she'd been a year ago. She went to work each day knowing her baby was happy and safe in Jake's care. Of course, come fall all of that could change, but she was confident she had time to work out a good childcare solution. She refused to think about whether or not Daisy might be old enough to miss her father when he left.

When Daisy woke from her afternoon nap, Violet fed and changed her, then strapped her into her car seat. Jake had gone on ahead to get his friend's studio set up.

"We're going to take pictures here against the plain backdrop, and then I have a surprise for you." He led her into the center of the circle of lights and made adjustments while she sat on the floor and undressed the baby.

"We're ready, but what are we supposed to do?" To her horror, the nervous laugh she'd worked so hard to banish had reappeared. She was used to cameras and photo sessions, but not while wearing snug, revealing clothing and holding her baby. Or with a man she'd slept with as the photographer.

"Just play with Daisy. Act natural."

Nothing about the situation felt natural, but she picked Daisy up under her arms and held her up in front of her with their faces inches apart. "I feel silly, kiddo, how about you?" She was rewarded with a burst of laughter, which never failed to make her laugh, too.

"That's it, you're loosening up. Whatever you do, keep making eye contact with her."

Although she loved Daisy and being a mother, playing did not come naturally to Violet. She had no younger siblings, and she'd never babysat. When she saw how comfortable Jake was making silly faces at Daisy or bouncing and nuzzling her, she was jealous. But she tried doing the things she saw him do, and the baby's response egged her on. After a few minutes she forgot all about Jake and his camera.

"Okay, we don't want to wear her out," he said after about fifteen minutes. "I think I got some great shots." He put his camera down and took Daisy from her. "Are you ready for the surprise?"

"Jake, you should probably know this about me. I hate surprises."

He laughed. "You know, I guessed that about you. But there's nothing to be afraid of. Just relax and trust me."

"The last time I did that . . ."

"You got the best surprise of all." He kissed Daisy's plump cheek. "Now go into the dressing room and change."

"Into what?" She pulled the curtain aside and saw he'd brought her favorite summer sundress. It was airy and sleeveless, with an allover floral print inspired by the paintings of Monet. Whenever she wore it, she felt beautiful and happy. "I don't suppose you brought shoes?"

He handed her a plastic bag. Inside were her matching lilac peep-toe sandals. "You won't need them once we get there, but you can't drive barefoot."

"Jake, are you going to tell me where we're going?"

He put Daisy on a table and began to dress her in a bright pink romper he pulled from another bag, a shower gift from her mother. "Violet, can't you ever just be spontaneous?"

"Spontaneous?" Jake had said the magic word. She remembered the night of the party, and her resolve to loosen up. There had been few opportunities in the past year, but maybe it was time to give it another try. "All right. I can be ready in two minutes."

He had Violet drive a few blocks and pull into the driveway of a venerable Boston homestead. She turned and stared at him. "Are we having high tea with the mayor?"

"The head of the garden society lives here, and we have permission to use her garden."

A uniformed maid led them behind the house to an enclosed garden that was a riot of colors and aromas. Violet, holding Daisy, headed for the mounds of roses, every shade from the palest pink to the richest crimson, and inhaled deeply. "I didn't think roses had such a strong scent."

"The ones you get from a florist don't." Jake was snapping off shots as Violet moved from one section of the garden to another.

"Sit in the grass over there, by the irises."

She laughed. "In spite of my name, I don't know much about

flowers. That's my mother's arena." She moved to the spot he indicated, and settled on the ground with Daisy on her lap.

Jake stooped down and pulled off her sandals, then spread her skirt out around her. He used both hands to tuck her hair behind her ears, then let his hands trail down the sides of her neck. She shivered. An instant later he was taking pictures again as though nothing had happened. Had the touch been accidental?

After ten minutes and two changes of position, Daisy started to get fidgety. Jake was working hard to coax a smile out of her when his cell phone rang. He frowned at the display.

"I have to take this."

He walked several feet away, but Violet overheard some of the conversation.

"If it has to be today, then it does. We'll make it work." Then he turned away and she couldn't make out the words. As he walked back in her direction, she heard, "he won't find out, trust me."

By the time he snapped the phone shut and returned it to his pocket, Daisy was crying.

"I think she's overstimulated," she said to Jake.

He shrugged. "I think we're done here. Something has come up that I have to handle. What time is your date tonight?"

He said the word "date" in a mocking way that Violet didn't care for. "Seven-thirty, but I'll need to get ready. If you could be back by seven . . ."

"No problem." He was packing away the cameras, his mind already someplace else.

She slid her shoes on. "Jake, is something wrong? Is it your uncle?"

He glanced over at her, but seemed not to notice she was having difficulty getting up off the ground while holding Daisy. "Everything's fine." He hoisted his camera bag over his shoulder and headed for the car, leaving her to struggle behind him with the crying baby.

*

At seven o'clock that evening, Violet was giving Daisy her bottle in the living room and wondering who would show up first, Jake or Richard. It would take her at least half an hour to dress, although she knew Richard wouldn't complain if he had to wait. She just didn't like leaving the two men alone together to butt heads like two bulls in a pen.

What was that all about, anyway? She knew Richard was jealous because he was in love with her, and saw Jake as a threat. But why was Jake so territorial? The obvious answer was Daisy. He didn't even know his child existed a month ago, but now that he did, he didn't want to share her. His caveman behavior didn't have anything to do with *her*. Or did it?

She remembered the way his fingers had touched her neck earlier, almost a caress, and how her heart had threatened to beat its way out of her chest. But then he ran off, with no explanation. Now he was late, which wasn't like him. In the week he'd been Daisy's nanny — she supposed it would be more accurate to say they were co-parenting her — she'd come to rely on his calm and competence. Which she knew was a mistake. Very soon he would be calm and competent halfway across the world.

A key turned in the lock, and Jake rushed in without warning. "Sorry, sorry, but I'm only a few minutes late, right?"

Daisy spit the nipple out of her mouth and lifted her head to smile at Jake.

"Here, let me give her the rest." He took the baby from her. "I'm sure you'll want to go put on a lot of make-up for your date with Rayburn . . . I mean, Richard."

Violet glared at him, then headed upstairs. When she got to her bedroom she realized she still had the burp cloth slung over her shoulder, and hadn't told him the baby should be burped before she got the rest of the bottle. Oh well, he was a natural at this baby stuff. He'd figure it out, right?

Wrong. She returned to the living room just in time to watch as he took the bottle away from Daisy and began to lift her to his shoulder. As soon as her head was upright, the baby burped and released the last couple ounces of formula all over the front of Jake's sky-blue polo shirt.

"Thank you, Daisy." She smiled back at him as though he'd meant it, and Violet had to admire his low-key reaction. "I'm not crazy about this formula," he said to her.

"I know, I think we might need to make a switch." Daisy had rarely spit up the breast milk, but they'd been getting baptized with the sour-smelling formula regularly for the past few days. She took the baby from him and set her down on the play mat. "Give me your shirt. I have a basket full of her things that are almost as nasty, and I'll throw in a load."

He removed the shirt by rolling it up from the bottom, already an old pro at handling messes. While the shirt was over his head and he couldn't see her, she let her gaze linger on his chest, the muscles rippling with his movement. She had no idea what Richard's chest and abs were like, and unfortunately, she had no interest in finding out.

When she returned her attention to his face, his wry expression and raised eyebrow told her he'd caught her staring. "I thought you might have gotten some on you," she explained, taking the shirt from him and walking away before he could see her blush.

In the laundry room she dumped detergent and a pile of Daisy's minuscule clothes into the washer, then gingerly turned Jake's shirt right-side out. As she was about to toss it in with the rest of the load, she noticed a folded sheet of paper in the breast pocket. Pink and thin, she thought it was a duplicate copy or a receipt. Although she planned to give it to him, she couldn't resist opening the folds and taking a peek first. It was a receipt from a hotel, dated today.

"I think I have a clean shirt in here . . ." Jake said from the doorway.

It was too late to hide what she was doing. Their eyes met and the doorbell rang at the same moment.

"This must be yours," she said, holding out the receipt. As though there could be another explanation for its presence in his pocket.

He took it without a word, grabbed a clean T-shirt, and left.

When she returned to the living room, Jake, still shirtless, was opening the door for Richard. He held out his hand to the new arrival, who grimaced like he was being offered a dead fish to hold.

"Don't let me keep you from . . . dressing, old man." Richard's eyes scanned Violet as though he was checking to see if she might have also been undressed a moment before.

"Just let me say goodbye to Daisy." Violet lifted the baby from the play mat but was careful not to jostle her. "As soon as Jake is ready, we can go."

"All set." Jake finished straightening his shirt and took the baby from her. "You two have a good time."

"Thanks." She picked up her purse off the table in the foyer and took Richard's arm. "I plan to have a *very* good time."

Richard's fervent puppy-dog expression when he opened the passenger door of his Lexus for her told her she'd gone too far baiting Jake. Her "date" reminded her of Brandon Gillette the night of the Junior Prom, leering at her as soon as they were alone, letting her know he expected to get lucky. Richard had about as much chance as Brandon did, no matter how angry she was at Jake.

"I made reservations at À La Mode," Richard told her as the car hummed to life.

"Lovely." She leaned her head back against the plush headrest. Much classier than taking her to some no-tell motel on the outskirts of town for a quickie.

But what did it matter to her how or where Jake scratched his sexual itches? Or with whom? It would be laughable to imagine he hadn't had another sex partner in the past year, just because *she* hadn't. Perhaps that was the problem. Remembering the way he'd touched her neck earlier, she could almost feel it burn. The reason was simple, now that she thought about it. Her sex drive was returning after the pregnancy, and Jake was an attractive man who she happened to know was very skilled at pleasing a woman.

He was always around her house, usually wearing cargo shorts that revealed his powerful legs, and with all the shirt changing, his naked chest was on display half a dozen times a day. If she thought he had romantic feelings for her, or even just sexual ones, it was wishful thinking brought about by surging hormones. He, obviously, had other outlets for his urges.

Well, so did she. Right at this moment she was on her way to Boston's best French restaurant with a handsome, sophisticated, and educated man. Just because there hadn't been chemistry between them in the past didn't mean it couldn't develop, did it?

Richard placed his hand on hers and made her jump. "You're quiet tonight. Worried about Daisy?"

"Not at all. Jake is extremely competent. When Daisy had her cold, I would have had no idea what to do if he hadn't been there."

Richard frowned, casting a quick glance at her before returning his gaze to the road. "Violet, give me a break. Something as simple as a cold wouldn't have been a problem for you. I've seen you interview slimy welfare defrauders and make them cry."

She laughed. "Yes, but with Daisy the goal is to make her stop." Richard couldn't understand how intimidating a twelve-pound person could be when she was solely dependent on you for her survival. "Jake is a real genius at that, I don't know how he . . ."

"You don't want to spend the whole evening talking about Macintyre . . . Jake, do you?"

"No, of course not." She didn't want to spend it *thinking* about him, either, but that was proving to be more difficult than she'd expected.

He gave her hand a squeeze and removed his, finally. She felt a film of sweat where it had been resting, and realized Richard, self-possessed and confident in every situation, was nervous. Because of her. It was very sweet and flattering, and she resolved to be kind to him.

For the next few hours, she focused on Richard as she would on the subject of an interview, forcing her mind away from maddening thoughts of Jake whenever they intruded. Richard was at his charming best, the food and wine were delicious, and at the end of the evening she had to admit she'd had a good time.

"We should do this every week," he said as she slipped her key into the lock.

She considered inviting him inside, could almost feel his longing to spend more time with her, but she knew Jake would be up. Still, she didn't want him to lose hope entirely.

"It was a lovely evening." She took a step toward him, which surprised him so much he lost his balance and might have fallen off the step if she hadn't grabbed his elbow.

"Oh!" He leaned forward, drew her gently against his chest, and pressed his lips against hers.

Like the rest of the evening, it was better than she expected it to be. They'd been coworkers and friends for so long, she was afraid it would be like kissing her brother. But it was nice, even though sparks didn't fly like when she kissed . . .

"Jake," Richard said as he removed his lips from hers.

She pulled back, confused. "Excuse me?"

"He turned on the porch light. What a jerk."

Once again she was reminded of prom night, and had to laugh.

"Violet, it isn't funny. The man is impertinent."

It wasn't the first time she'd noticed that when Richard was angry, the timbre of his voice changed from well-modulated to prissy. Not an attractive trait in a man.

"Well, I can't fire him, but he won't be around forever." She turned the key. "Goodnight, Richard."

*

Jake was annoyed when he pulled up to the portico of the hotel on the outskirts of the city where he'd left Carrie the previous day and didn't see her waiting. It would be better for both of them, he'd told her, if he could make a quick in and out. But a downpour had begun on his way there, perfectly suited to his foul mood, and he couldn't blame her for staying dry in the lobby.

So he was startled when his rear passenger-side door opened. The woman he'd seen huddled under a black umbrella was in fact Carrie, with her long blonde hair wrapped in a scarf and her blue eyes hidden by sunglasses, despite the rain. She threw her suitcase and wet umbrella in the backseat before climbing in the front with him, her head on a swivel the whole time.

He had to laugh in spite of his impatience. "Welcome to the Witness Protection Program. What should I call you now?"

She didn't smile or even remove the sunglasses as he pulled away from the building. A glimpse at the bruises on her forearm and her chewed-up fingernails reminded him this was deadly serious to her. He'd been annoyed at having to cut his afternoon with Violet and Daisy short yesterday, when Carrie called and told him in a whispery voice he could hardly hear that her boyfriend had fallen asleep after making drunken threats. She believed she was in serious danger if she didn't get out of the apartment immediately. Based on his memories of Ellsworth and his mother, he'd had to agree.

Although he would have had time to take her all the way to Wickham, and Uncle Matt would probably not have minded her arriving a day early, he'd been so excited about his photo session with Violet and Daisy he couldn't wait to develop the pictures. As soon as he'd assessed Carrie's injuries and determined she didn't need medical attention, he dropped her at a hotel far enough from her boyfriend to give her an illusion of safety, then hurried back to the city and his friend's darkroom. A bad decision, as it turned out.

The pictures were even more spectacular than he'd hoped, and he stopped thinking about time as he worked with them. When he got back to Violet's, a few minutes late, he was so jazzed up he jostled Daisy and ended up with regurgitated formula all over him. Which led to Violet's discovery of the hotel receipt.

Of course he knew what she thought, and the way she'd sneered at him made her opinion of men who checked into hotel rooms in the middle of the day all too clear. But if he told her he was helping Carrie, the consequences would be far worse. She wasn't going to banish him from Daisy's life for having sleazy sex, not if he was discreet, but if she knew he'd even spoken to the former nanny, she'd take him to court. He could even lose the right to see his daughter.

Helping this woman, who was nothing to him, wasn't worth the risk. He glanced over at Carrie, who had finally taken off the glasses. Tears slid from her eyes.

"I can't thank you enough for helping me."

Mentally, he agreed. "If I hadn't, you would have had to go to a shelter, that's all."

She shook her head. "Joe knows about those places. He'd have found me."

"I don't see how he can find you at my Uncle Matt's." Out of the corner of his eye, he saw her put a finger in her mouth, even though she had no nails left to bite.

"What if your uncle doesn't like me?" Her voice, as usual, was nearly a whisper.

He smiled, knowing his uncle had never met a woman as pretty as Carrie and not liked her. In the close proximity of the car, he noticed fine lines around her eyes for the first time and realized she was not as young as he'd first thought. Well within Matt's age range for women, which was wide. He'd have to remind him she was there to work for him, and anything else would be inappropriate.

"Just do your job, and you won't have to worry about a thing," he told her. Except for what she was going to do when Matt was well enough to go back to work. But with any luck, he'd be in Peru by then and his uncle could take over as her knight in shining armor.

Matt, however, was lacking not only in chivalry when he greeted Carrie forty minutes later, but in normal good manners.

"You're the babysitter? A fine day it is when these whippersnapper boys think I need a caretaker." He ignored Carrie's outstretched hand and swiveled the wheelchair so his back was to her. Jake was relieved to see his skill at maneuvering the thing had improved, at least.

"Whippersnapper? Carrie, believe it or not, my uncle is, what? Forty-eight?"

"Forty-*seven*."

"He must be watching too many episodes of *Little House on the Prairie*." She marched over to the television and hit the power button. "First thing we need to do is find the Wickham library." She surveyed the wreckage of the room with her hands on her hips.

Jake, already confused by his uncle's cold reception to an attractive woman, was newly amazed by Carrie's assertiveness. The further they got from Boston, he realized, the less she had seemed like a frightened, cowering victim.

He scrutinized her for the first time, and saw what his uncle did. A woman of medium height and indeterminate age, wearing baggy jeans and an oversized black football jersey. The three-quarter sleeves concealed most, but not all, of her bruises. Although he knew Carrie was slender, her outfit was hiding her more-than-adequate curves, and the blonde hair, usually his uncle's weakness, was completely covered. Well, he had a surprise in store, unless she was planning to make this outfit her work uniform.

She began to pick up the empty beer cans and food containers strewn about the room, and when she passed close to Matt's wheelchair he reached out and took her wrist. Although she flinched, Jake knew his uncle's touch had been firm but gentle.

"You seem like a smart girl. Maybe a little bossy. So tell me, why would you let some . . . jerk do this to you?"

Carrie didn't need to follow Matt's gaze to the bruised on her arm to know what he was talking about. She stared him straight in the eye and answered in the strong voice that was still a wonder to Jake.

"You can't understand, a man like you. I just met you, but already I know you say what you think. Joe was a real charmer at first, he treated me better than any man before him. After he had me hooked, he showed himself for what he really is. Evil."

After a moment, Matt released her wrist. She continued to stare him down. "You're right. I can't understand a man like that. But you'll be safe here, I promise."

She shook her head. "You can't make that promise. But if you can give me a job, and some distance from . . . him, that will be enough."

He nodded, and she turned and headed for the kitchen with the trash in her arms. "Here, let me help you." He did a quick turn with the chair and followed her, glancing back over his shoulder once.

"Jake, what are you still doing here?"

Chapter Nine

Violet told herself what Jake did during his private time was none of her business, but she blushed and found herself unable to speak to him on Sunday morning when they met in the kitchen. What if he tried to explain? But she didn't have to worry. He told her he had a lot of work to catch up on, and asked if she'd mind getting up with Daisy for the rest of the week. After she'd stormed into the nursery and insisted on it the first day, she couldn't very well refuse, although she had to double her caffeine consumption to stay awake through the late news.

For the next week their paths crossed only when they came and left the house, and their only conversation was about Daisy. That was just fine with her.

Then, on Saturday morning, she woke with the sun higher than normal and knew Jake must have gotten up with the baby. The nursery was empty, so she followed the smell of cinnamon down to the kitchen.

He was whisking eggs in a bowl, and a pan of cinnamon buns was cooling on the counter. Daisy was in her infant seat, a film of dried rice cereal around her mouth. When she saw her mother, the rattle she was holding went flying and her arms waved with frantic longing.

"Good morning, cutie." She undid Daisy's safety strap and lifted her up, kissing her plump, sticky cheeks. "Baking is one of your many talents, I see."

Jake turned and smiled. "I figure the first part of that sentence was directed to Daisy, and the second part to me. Although the first part could have been meant for either of us. The recipe came from your only cookbook, which was apparently unused until today."

"A gift from my mother, who thinks all women should know how to cook. In theory, I agree." Bacon sizzled in the frying pan.

"You're eating meat?"

He shrugged. "I saw it in the refrigerator, and I didn't want you to risk the dangers of meat consumption alone."

He poured coffee into her favorite mug, added milk and sugar the way she liked it, and set it on the table. There was a package on her placemat wrapped in familiar gift wrap. After a moment she recognized it as the paper she'd used for Seth and Jenna's anniversary gift.

"Is the paper a coincidence, or have you discovered where I keep my gift wrap supplies, too?"

"Everyone keeps their gift wrap in the hall closet." Jake removed the pan from the flame and reached for Daisy so her hands would be free. "Open it."

Violet sipped her coffee, stalling. Although she was the world's most extravagant giver of gifts, she hated to receive them. Seth theorized it was because of Monty. His gifts were always over-the-top, but never the thing they wanted when they wanted it. A foreign doll for Violet dressed in an authentic wedding costume when she wanted a Barbie like all the other girls; a set of drums for Seth when he wanted skis. Afterwards, when her father was gone again, she secretly believed it was because she hadn't been grateful enough for his gifts. She swore that next time, she would love whatever he brought her, or at least convince him that she did.

When she confessed this to her mother after Monty's funeral, she shook her head and put her arms around her. "He never even noticed whether you liked the gift or not. It wasn't about you."

"Will you just open the thing? Our eggs are getting cold." Although he acted like it wasn't a big deal, she was enough of an actress herself to see what he was trying to hide. Whether or not she liked the gift was important to Jake.

She flipped it over so she could slide her fingers under the taped edge, revealing the back of a picture frame. Now that she knew what it was, she was excited, and relieved. Turning it over revealed a black and white image of her and Daisy, gazing into each other's eyes with delighted smiles.

"Oh! It's beautiful." Somehow he had captured visually the intimate connection she had with her baby. "Every day I think about how precious this time with her is, and how fleeting. But I'll always have this one moment. Thank you."

He nodded. "You're welcome. Those aren't tears, are they?"

Laughing and crying at once, she blotted her eyes with a paper napkin. "I know the first time was an accident, but you've given me the two best gifts of my life."

*

Although the door to Violet's spacious dressing room at the television studio was half open, Seth knocked on it before sticking his head in. He had business in the city on Monday, and had decided to fly in on Friday night and spend the weekend with her and Daisy.

She rose from the vanity chair and gave him a big hug. "You didn't have to meet me here, you know, you could have gone to the house. You're probably exhausted from traveling all day."

"And let your child's psycho father yank me around by the front of my shirt? No thanks. Besides, being tired will help me get to sleep at a decent East coast hour tonight. I brought dinner." He held up a bag from the deli on the first floor of her building. "Clam chowder and lobster rolls."

Violet took the bag and sat down on the plush sofa, spreading the food out on the coffee table while Seth removed his jacket and draped it over the vanity chair. He whistled and picked up a smaller reproduction of the picture Jake had given her two weeks ago.

"Psycho Dad took this?"

"*Jake* took it. It's wonderful, isn't it? He had a large one framed and hung it in the nursery."

"I've flipped through his books in the bookstore, so I knew he was good. This isn't like his other work, of course." His gaze flicked between Violet and the photograph. "He really captured you. The you *I* know, but most people don't."

His comment made her laugh. "How do you know what other people think of me?"

He returned the picture to the vanity and sat beside her. "You present a very cool and professional demeanor to the world. It's appropriate for what you do. The question is, of course, why you chose your career. It's like you're hiding in plain sight." He gestured toward the muted television monitor on the wall.

"Thank you, Doctor Freud. But I guess the secret me is about to be revealed to the world."

"What do you mean?" He sank his teeth into the lobster roll. "Mmm, I do love the food in this town."

"I told you about the exhibit of Jake's work we're going to see tomorrow. He asked my permission to show some of the pictures he took of me and Daisy, and I agreed. Apparently his agent thinks he has a real talent for photographing mothers and children."

"Not all of the children are his, I hope." He uncovered the steaming container of soup.

Violet resisted the urge to throw a spoon at him, having had similar thoughts herself. What did she really know about Jake, after all? Although, as it turned out, she was going to have the perfect opportunity to learn more.

"Returning to the subject of my career, which you seem to think is all about appearances, I feel like I'm moving forward again, finally."

She'd had many tearful conversations with Seth toward the end of her pregnancy and in the first weeks after Daisy was born, complaining that she felt like she was on autopilot and couldn't concentrate on anything but her baby.

"You're more comfortable leaving Daisy, then?"

She shrugged. Just the phrase "leaving Daisy" was still enough to pull sudden tears into her eyes. "I'd like to have more time with her, sure. I'm missing a lot. But I know she's happy with Jake, and he's great at keeping me involved. She rolled over for the first time the other day, or at least I thought it was the first time. Jake made a big deal out of it, but I think he'd already seen her do it."

"Nice. But when he deserts you again, you're back to square one in the nanny situation."

Once again she and her twin were following the same thought track. Although she knew his use of the word "desert" was unfair, it was often the way she felt, too. But Jake hadn't volunteered to become a father, and she'd made no attempt to involve him in the process. She supposed she should just be grateful for the help he'd given her.

"We found a lovely older woman in the neighborhood who's been doing some babysitting when Jake has to work during the day, and I think she could be convinced to take the job permanently."

"What's changed with your job?"

"When I was hired, we discussed special projects I might do, but everything got put on hold because of my maternity leave. Not to mention my lack of enthusiasm when I came back." She got up and walked to her vanity table to check her make-up and hair. In another half hour she'd have to begin preparations for the late newscast. "Yesterday I asked my boss if I could begin the interview segment we talked about then."

"He said yes, I assume."

She grimaced at Seth's image in the mirror. "He said yes, but he wanted to pick my first subject."

"And?"

"I'm going to interview a famous photojournalist. His name is Jake Macintyre."

*

Seth slung the diaper bag over his shoulder while Violet pushed the stroller into the posh uptown gallery the next afternoon. "It takes a real man to carry a pink bag with an embroidered teddy bear on it," he told her. "I bet Psycho Dad wouldn't do it."

"Oh, but he does," she said, wincing at the nickname. Since Seth was using it to goad her, correcting him again would just add to his fun. "I've never seen a man less concerned about what other people think of him. Present company included."

His grin was wide as he held the door for her. "Are you ready to meet your in-laws?"

Fortunately, the first "in-law" they saw had a friendly and familiar face, although it was disconcerting to see his large body crammed into a wheelchair. "Violet Gallagher," Matt's big voice boomed so everyone could hear, "let me see that baby!"

The only way to accomplish that was to take Daisy out of the stroller, but she'd just napped and eaten, and seemed agreeable to all the handling and fuss. Until she was put onto the lap of the big man, when she started to wail.

"Mommy's right here." Violet hoped she wouldn't have to offend her friend by snatching the baby right back.

Daisy, however, despite the tears, seemed mesmerized by her great-uncle. When he began to talk to her in an uncharacteristically hushed, high voice and make comic faces, she quieted within seconds.

"Silliness must be a family trait," Seth whispered to Violet.

Despite being preoccupied with Daisy, Matt heard him. "You must be Violet's brother. Excuse me if I don't shake hands, what with the baby and the cast on my leg and all. You've met Jake, I take it?"

Seth laughed. "The first time we met, he tried to kill me. Last night he was much more civil."

"Hmm, sounds like Jake. Not the civil part, the other thing."

To Violet's relief, Jake had apologized for manhandling Seth, and her brother had shrugged it off. In fact, they'd stayed up long after she went to bed, Jake sharing tips with her brother on photographing children with a digital camera. At least that's what they were talking about when she went upstairs. If there'd been any discussion of her or Daisy, Seth hadn't mentioned it.

Matt lifted Daisy over his head and swooped and dipped her in a way Violet found alarming. The baby seemed to love it, but after he coaxed a sudden giggle out of her, he hooted so loudly that her face crumpled and she began to cry again. He brought her back down to his lap, but he seemed to be out of distraction tactics and his frown made her cry even harder.

Violet came to his rescue. "I think I'll put her back in the stroller so we can look at Jake's pictures."

Matt passed her to Violet with obvious relief. "Jake's around somewhere. He and his agent are giving a personal tour to some big shots. You just missed Jamie, although he'll be at the dinner tonight."

"Oh, I'm not going to that." At breakfast Jake had invited them to the dinner party his agent was hosting after the show, but she'd already made plans with Richard. As usual, she had mixed feelings about choosing Richard over Jake. It was the sensible choice, but not the most appealing.

As for Jamie, Jake had brought the baby to his apartment so he could "meet" his new niece, but Violet hadn't met him yet. She knew Pamela, of course, and hoped Jamie wouldn't hold it against her that she'd fired his girlfriend.

"I don't think Pamela will be there," Matt said, as though he had psychic abilities. Nothing would surprise her about the man. "I don't think she'll be around at all much longer." His grin told her he wouldn't be sorry. "Come on, I'll give you a tour."

He made a sharp turn with the chair and headed into the first alcove, where large black and white photographs hung in stark contrast against a creamy white wall. Seth took the handles of the stroller and headed off on his own.

"Jake told me he and Jamie were trying to find someone to help you while you recover from your injury," she said to Matt. "How did that work out?"

He gave her a sly wink. "I have such a great nurse I'm hoping I can keep her. I may just keep this cast on forever."

The idea of this vigorous man consigning himself to a wheelchair for a woman made her laugh, but a glance at Jake's work sobered her. The picture in front of her depicted a plain building that might have been an orphanage. In front of it, a nun dressed in white was surrounded by a group of children, all either naked or wearing ragged scraps of clothing. They were engaged in a game involving sticks and stones, their faces full of intense concentration.

The photograph evoked conflicting emotions in her. The children were bones and hollows, their toys scavenged from nature. They had no parents. But there was loving benevolence in the nun's expression, and optimism in their play.

Absorbed in Jake's work now, she went from picture to picture. The rest of the black-and-white group was all of children, some with their mothers, and portrayed hope in the midst of poverty and despair. She turned a corner and found color photographs of scenic places, but each had a humanizing touch. An outbuilding, a crumbled rock wall, a rusted farming implement. Some sign that man had been there and left his mark.

"His work will never be in *National Geographic*," a familiar voice said behind her. "There's no sense of grandeur. He can't get away from the extraneous details." She recognized Richard's voice before she turned around.

"Extraneous details like starving children?"

He shrugged. "You didn't tell me you were going to be here today."

"Jake's a friend. Of course I came to see his work."

"Is he a *friend*, Violet?" His face was contorted, unattractive.

"Richard, this isn't the place . . ."

He lowered his voice and leaned closer. "Because we've been seeing each other for a while now, Violet, and you say you care about me. But you're always rushing off. I think it's time we took our relationship further, if you know what I mean."

Her face flushed. There was no mistaking what he meant.

"Jake is staying at your house. Why can't you spend the night with me?"

"You must have forgotten my brother's visiting. He's going out to dinner with us tonight, while Grace Cornelius baby-sits." That put off the decision for now, but Violet knew Richard wasn't going to let the subject drop.

"Violet, you didn't tell me you were bringing a friend." Jake was suddenly at her side, slipping his arm around her waist. He reached his hand out to Richard, who was forced to shake it. "I hope you're enjoying the show. But I think you'll like what's in the other room best. Why don't you take a look while I have a word with Violet?"

Richard had no choice but to go where Jake indicated.

"Did you really want to talk to me, or did you just want to get rid of him?" Violet, suddenly weary, sank onto a bench in the center of the small room. Jake sat beside her.

"I wondered what you thought of my work."

She was about to say that her opinion couldn't possibly matter, but the frown on his face told her it mattered very much. Despite the success of the books, the crowd at the show today, and the respect of his peers, was it possible he still needed reassurance?

"I expected it to be beautiful. I didn't expect it to be so emotional. So thought-provoking."

Richard strode back in, and stood in front of them with his arms crossed. He glared at Jake.

"I think Rayburn found the pictures in the other room thought-provoking," he said.

"So. That's how it is." There was both anger and resignation in his tone.

Violet looked from one man to the other. "Richard, what are you talking about?"

His gaze went to her. "I don't know what kind of game you're playing with me, but it's over."

Although he was obviously waiting for a response, Violet was bewildered and said nothing.

"So I'll just . . . go," he finally said.

When Richard was no longer in sight, Violet turned back to Jake. "Do you know what that was all about? More importantly, are we still invited for dinner? It seems I no longer have plans."

Jake's smile was impish. "No, and yes."

Seth came toward them. Daisy was blowing bubbles and staring at her hand in the stroller, but when she saw her mother, she lifted her head and strained forward.

"Okay, darling girl, I'll carry you for awhile."

"Violet, you really need to come into the other room now that the crowd has thinned a bit," her brother said. "Your show is a smash, Jake."

Jake shrugged. "The new work is generating quite a buzz."

Violet was stunned by the new work, two walls of the photographs he'd taken of her and Daisy. She hadn't seen any of the pictures he'd taken in the garden, and she was impressed. Instead of the vivid colors she'd expected, he'd done something to mute and soften them, so the overall effect was similar to French Impressionist paintings.

While the pictures from the garden shoot seemed to be all about composition and color, the black and white series was pure emotion. The love between Violet and Daisy was paramount.

She pulled her gaze away long enough to turn to Jake.

His eyes were shining. "Do you like them?"

"Very much," was all she could think to say. A silver-haired woman wearing flowing white garments came and pulled Jake away by his elbow, and Seth took his place beside her. He raised his eyebrows in the familiar way that meant he was implying something. Usually she knew what it was, but not today.

"What? They're beautiful, aren't they?"

"They are, but I don't think you're seeing the third party in these pictures."

"What do you mean?" Daisy was squirming, and they might have to leave soon.

"Jake is in all the pictures he takes, in one way or another. It's what gives them their emotional power. These pictures are screaming to me that either he's in love with you, you're in love with him, or both."

"What a silly idea!"

"Why?"

"It just is." Violet was annoyed and growing agitated. Daisy felt it, and began to whimper. "Jake loves Daisy, yes. And he's a great photographer. If he took your picture, people might think he was in love with *you*."

Seth laughed and took Daisy from her. "I think it's time we got Daisy home, don't you?"

With Daisy crying, and Seth walking away, there was nothing more she could say. Even if she had the opportunity, she wasn't sure what it would be. Seth was a smart guy, and his conclusions were usually correct. But not this time.

Jake saw her leaving and waved. "I'll call you about tonight." He couldn't seem to stop smiling. At her? Or because his show was such a huge success?

*

Jamie and Jake arrived at Millie's downtown apartment at almost the same moment, and their hostess directed them to the bar. "Fix yourselves drinks, dear boys, while I see to the catering. I have the most wonderful announcement to make, but I'm going to wait until everyone gets here!"

"What do you think it is?" Jamie asked as he uncapped the Scotch. "One of your Madonna pictures of Violet and Daisy sold for a million dollars?"

Jake grinned as he poured himself a glass of soda. "I see you're dateless tonight."

"Let's just say you can move back in anytime you want." He grimaced before sampling his drink.

"Sorry." Jake wasn't surprised, although Pamela had stuck around longer than most.

"Although you'd be crazy to leave your cozy setup."

It was Jake's turn to twist his face into a frown. "I wouldn't call it a 'cozy setup.' I'm taking care of my daughter."

"First thing I thought when I saw those pictures today was, 'Jake's in love with her.'"

"Just wait until you have a kid." Although the only way he could imagine that happening was by accident, the same way it had happened to him.

Jamie laughed and clapped his brother on the back. "I was talking about Violet."

"I'm not in love with Violet."

Uncle Matt rolled his wheelchair into the room at that moment, followed by Millie. "Hell, yes, you are!"

"I don't know what you boys are talking about, but fix your charming uncle a drink, Jake." Millie passed him in a cloud of expensive-smelling perfume and placed a tray of appetizers on a low table.

Without even asking what he'd like, Jake uncapped a beer and handed it to Matt. "Listen, let's not pursue this insanity. Violet and her brother will be here any minute, and I wanted to ask you about Carrie before she gets here. Is she working out?"

"Ah, Carrie." He took a long swallow of the Sam Adams. "My future wife."

Jake almost spewed his own drink. "I brought her to Wickham to be your housekeeper."

Matt pointed his beer bottle at Jake, who was afraid it was going to spill on Millie's Oriental rug. "I'm not in denial about who I love. Unfortunately, unlike your Violet, Carrie doesn't return my feelings. Yet."

The doorbell rang again, and Jake found himself holding his breath as he waited to hear Violet's voice. But no, he wasn't in love with her. Right. As his mother used to say, you can lie to everyone else, but you can't lie to yourself.

In this situation, he couldn't even lie to everyone else. Why had he sent Rayburn to see the pictures of Violet and the baby? Because he'd known what he would see. And if Rayburn could see it, then anyone could. Had Violet? He'd have to do some damage control, and pronto. Because Violet didn't love *him*. And even if the sparks they'd felt the night they met could be coaxed into a three-alarm blaze, what would it accomplish? He couldn't be the man she desired and deserved.

That man would show up someday, and when he did, Jake would be happy for Violet. He would even try to be mature and share his daughter with the guy. It just wasn't going to be Richard Rayburn. Jake would make certain of that.

Chapter Ten

"Here's the other star of the show," Millie said to Violet, who was hovering on the threshold of the room with her brother behind her. She grabbed her by the shoulders and air-kissed both her cheeks.

Jake stepped forward. "Violet, the woman pretending to kiss you is Millie Winston, my agent."

"And you're the handsome brother," Millie turned to Seth and repeated the greeting.

"I'm the other handsome brother, Jamie."

His brother extended his hand first to Violet, holding it longer than Jake thought he should, and then to Seth.

"Enough of all this kissing and greeting. Now that everyone is here, I want to announce our wonderful news." Millie floated over to Jake and put her arm around his waist. "*Bébé*, the French company that makes those wonderful skin and hair products for babies and mothers, wants Jake to be the photographer for their new ad campaign."

Jake opened his mouth to ask her if she'd lost her mind, but she wasn't finished.

"There's more good news. They want Daisy and Violet to be their models!"

Jake watched Violet smile uncertainly when Millie delivered the first part of the announcement, but she appeared stunned by the second part. Her eyes met his with what he thought was a glare of accusation. How could Millie put them all on the spot like this? She knew he didn't do commercial work. If he wasn't making enough money for her, she could find herself another client. But he knew this wasn't the time or place to say so.

Everyone was staring at him, waiting for a clue. Was it good news or not?

"We'll have to discuss this later, Millie. I'm not sure it's my kind of gig, and Violet already has a job. As for Daisy, I didn't think we'd make her get a job for a few more years. Diapers aren't *that* expensive."

Everyone relaxed then, laughing at his joke. Except Violet. Millie's maid, dressed theatrically in a black-and-white uniform, entered and rang a little bell. The commission Millie made from his work allowed her to have this over-the-top lifestyle. Why were people always greedy for more?

"Let's go in to dinner," Millie trilled. If she was disappointed with Jake's response, she didn't show it.

In the dining room, Jake pulled out Violet's chair, which was to the left of his. "I'm so sorry." He spoke as softly as he could, so the others wouldn't hear. "This is the first I've heard about it. But don't worry, it will never happen."

She arranged the skirt of her dress around her as she settled into the chair. It was the same flowered dress she'd worn for the photo shoot, and it had the same effect on him as it had that day — it made him want to undo the row of tiny buttons down the front.

Her smile was thoughtful as she raised those beguiling blue eyes to his. "But I'd like to do it."

*

There was a sudden silence as Violet became the focus of everyone's attention. She looked around the table at the surprised faces. "I use *bébé* products, and I love them. They're made of natural ingredients, and the company is very green, very earth-friendly. I think it would be great fun to model for their ads."

Millie clapped her hands in delight. "I knew you'd do it! Daisy is so beautiful, you have a duty to share her with the world."

It wasn't like Violet to make a decision without careful reflection, which was why Seth was shooting her a "who are you and what have you done with my sister?" look from across the table. She was telegraphing back, "you're the one who told me to be spontaneous," even as she acknowledged that her sensible side had weighed in on the issue as well.

But she'd seen Jake's jaw stiffen when she said she wanted to do the ads, and knew her spontaneity had been a mistake. As usual, what worked for other people had failed to work for her. For some reason, as eager as he'd been to take the other photographs, Jake didn't want to do this project. He probably didn't want to spend the time with her it would require, since he was seeing someone else.

"Jake would have to agree, of course." She spoke without making eye contact with anyone, then sipped from an icy glass of water, hoping to calm the flush of embarrassment she was feeling.

"He doesn't like to do commercial work," Millie said, while the subject of the conversation poked at his salad with his fork. "But this wouldn't just be advertising, it would be art. It would also be a very limited contract. Jake will be leaving the country in several weeks, and Daisy is the right age."

"I think we should just enjoy this wonderful dinner right now, Mil," Jake said. "Violet and I will discuss it later."

She had until they got home to figure out what to say to him. A few hours posing for him, and she could set up a substantial college account for Daisy. Yes, she had a good job, and Jake was well off financially, if the crowd at his show was any indicator. But the future was uncertain, especially for Jake, who visited war zones and navigated dangerous terrain.

That would be a good argument to make. She'd wanted, and still did, to be independent. The decision to have the baby had been hers alone, so the financial responsibility should be hers too.

The subject remained dropped only until the maid cleared the salad plates and replaced them with the main course, lamb chops with baby vegetables.

"You know, Jake," Jamie said, "if you just did this one commercial job, it would expose your work to a lot more people. That company markets to mothers, but I've seen their ads in general interest publications."

"It would expose Daisy to a lot more people, too," Jake replied. "I'm not sure that's a good thing."

Violet's face burned. Was he implying she would do something that wasn't in her child's best interests? Jamie was staring at her from across the table, and their eyes met. He was so different from Jake, she would never have guessed they were brothers. Where Jake had the gold and bronze coloring of a California surfer, Jamie had the intensely dark hair and blue eyes peculiar to some people of Irish descent. Like her and Seth, but where their eyes were the color of the afternoon sky, his were the deep blue of the sky at dusk.

Jamie smiled at Violet, but his words were directed at Jake. "Isn't she exposed to the public right now, in the gallery?"

He raised his hand, palm forward, when Jake glowered at him. "You did that to share your artistry, the same way I want my buildings to be appreciated. But why not let *bébé* give your child a college fund at the same time?"

"Jamie, your brother asked you to stop talking about this baby company, whatever it is." Matt said in the voice of a father who's heard enough arguing. It was obvious this wasn't the first time he'd mediated between the brothers. "Why don't we move on to a safer topic, like religion or politics?"

*

When they got back to Violet's, Seth went upstairs to the guest room to call his wife, while Jake walked Grace Cornelius down the street to her house. Violet spent the time organizing the arguments she would use on Jake, even jotting down notes.

Her preparation turned out to be unnecessary.

"This is what Millie said *bébé* is offering," he said without preamble when he returned, handing her a slip of paper with a number followed by an amazing number of zeroes. "She can get more. If you weren't so eager to do it for some reason, I'd say no. But you are, and it does seem foolish to pass up the money. Jamie's right. It can go into a trust fund for Daisy, since you won't let me set one up otherwise. I'll know her future is secure."

He said something she didn't catch. "Hmm?" Her sofa was so comfortable and cushy. She was glad she hadn't gotten the stark, modern one Pamela had suggested.

"I think we both need to get some sleep."

This time she heard him, but as though from a great distance, and she found it impossible to reply. Sinking further into the cushions, she just smiled.

When her eyes blinked open again she saw, not her blue upholstery fabric, but Jake's cotton shirt. It was about an inch away, since her face was resting on his chest. The first thing she did was check to see if she'd not only used him as a pillow, but drooled on him as well. Mercifully, she had not.

She attempted to raise herself back into the position she'd started from, but discovered she couldn't move. Jake's left arm was around her, and it clutched her even more tightly when she tried to pull away. In order to shift at all, she'd have to push her hand against his chest for leverage.

As soon as she did, his eyelids fluttered open and his other arm went around her too. For a moment she panicked. An outdoorsman like Jake might wake up alert and ready to take action, and in his semi-conscious state, he could think she was some kind of threat. Both their bodies tensed for a moment, then she felt his relax. He grinned at her, then closed the gap between their faces, pressing his lips against hers.

She relaxed too, relieved she wasn't in danger. Then she realized she was just as "caught" as she'd been when she first woke up. If she pulled away now he would surely let her go, but how — and why — would she do that? Kissing Jake felt right, like something she'd lost had been returned to her. When their mouths opened and their tongues met, it felt more than right, it felt unstoppable. She was no longer thinking, only reacting to the heat and desire coursing through her.

Jake moved his right arm to the front of her dress and began to fumble with the buttons at her bodice. Knowing the combination of tiny buttons and thick masculine fingers would defeat him, she brought her own hands to the task. She was about to rip the dress down the front in frustration when his hand finally slipped inside her dress and the thin fabric of her bra. The heat and roughness of his calloused skin brought her to the brink of orgasm, and she gasped.

At the same moment, Jake froze. "Did you hear something?"

She struggled to quiet her ragged breathing. At first she heard only squawks of static coming from the baby monitor, then a whiny cry. "Daisy."

Jake sighed. "It sounds like she might go back to sleep."

But the mood was broken; Violet's brain was functioning again. What had she been thinking? That was the problem, she hadn't been thinking at all. She sat up and pulled the front of her dress together.

"I'll go check on her. Goodnight, Jake."

He put his hand on her arm, letting it slide away as she stood. Without his touch, the air felt cold. She shivered as she forced herself away from him and toward the stairs.

"Sleep well," he called after her in a husky voice.

*

Seth, despite the time zone difference, was already up and drinking coffee the next morning when Violet staggered into the kitchen carrying Daisy, followed a few minutes later by Jake, who appeared as bedraggled as she felt.

"Did Daisy have a bad night?" Seth placed a cup of coffee in front of his sister and took the baby from her. She squealed with delight and grabbed his nose. "She theems fine now, but the two of you look like you didn't get any sleep. Oww!"

Violet snuck a glance at Jake over the top of her coffee cup, but he didn't meet her eyes. "She was fine, but for some reason I didn't sleep well. After I fed her I took her into bed with me, but she just wanted to play."

"Well, it was a big day for all of you." Seth poured another cup with his free hand and set it in front of Jake. "Did you come to any agreement about the advertising offer?"

"We're going to do it, and put our profits into a trust fund for Daisy," Jake answered. "At least that's what I'm doing with my salary."

"Me too," Violet added. "Maybe you can handle the details for us, Seth?"

"I'd be glad too. And as the only fully functioning adult here this morning, I'll whip up some breakfast. Any takers?"

Jake checked his watch and groaned. "I'm supposed to meet Millie for brunch, and I'm going to be late."

"I accept." Violet slid her chair away from the table and stood. "As long as I can shower while you work your magic."

An hour later, Violet, feeling much fresher, had just stabbed her first bite of Seth's cinnamon French toast when the doorbell rang. Seth was shoveling applesauce into Daisy and it was clear she wouldn't tolerate an interruption, so she put the warm morsel in her mouth and chewed fast on her way to the front door.

Even so, she swallowed a bigger piece than she should have when she discovered Richard on her front step, sagging against the door frame like his bones had turned to jelly. She was speechless, not because she didn't expect to see him, but because she couldn't breathe.

"You don't want to see me, I know." He was wearing the hangdog face that used to soften her heart, but now just irritated her. "Nothing to say? You're right, I should just go."

She pulled on the back of his shirt as he turned away, believing herself in urgent need of the Heimlich maneuver. But just as he spun back around she managed to get the lump of bread unstuck and began to cough violently.

"Oh, Violet, you're choking!"

Richard stepped into the foyer and whacked her on the back, which only made her cough harder. Tears coursed down her cheeks. "Stop! I'm okay now."

Seth was there, holding Daisy, who was crying. "Rayburn? What did you do to my sister?"

What was it with men and the last name thing? "Everyone just relax." Violet's voice was still croaky, and Daisy was screaming full-force, so no one heard her. She took a deep breath. "Everyone be quiet!"

Even Daisy fell silent. "Richard and I need to talk. Seth, could you watch the baby while we walk over to the park for a few minutes?" Then she headed off down the sidewalk, giving Seth no choice but to do as she asked, and knowing Richard would follow her.

Violet didn't speak until she found an isolated bench where they could sit and talk without being disturbed. Although she hadn't known what Richard was prattling on about when he left the gallery the previous day, she realized later he'd seen the same thing in the pictures her brother had tried to point out to her. If it weren't for the kiss, she would tell Richard the same thing she told Seth — she and Jake did not have feelings for each other. Now she wasn't so sure.

"I know you think there's something going on between me and Jake," she began.

He shook his head and smiled. "What I think is that there's

nothing going on between you and me, and I came by today to ask you if there's a chance that will change. Jake will be going away soon, and he'll be gone for a long time."

She didn't like being reminded of Jake's departure, but she'd have to deal with it eventually. "I never meant to deceive you. You're such a great guy, and handsome, and you'd be a wonderful father. I was hoping . . ."

"For some chemistry to develop. But that isn't going to happen with Jake around."

She knew now it was *never* going to happen, and it wasn't fair to let Richard think otherwise. She reached for his hand. "I hope you'll always be my friend."

He sighed, and caught her hand between both of his. "You'll need someone to fix things for you while Macintyre is off traipsing the globe."

Thinking of Richard with tools made her roll her eyes and laugh, and he joined in. At least one of her relationships might turn out all right.

*

To Jake's amazement, the turnout at the gallery on Sunday was even bigger than the day before.

"It's the mother-daughter pictures," Millie told him. "I think a rumor has gotten out that the baby is yours."

Jake scowled, thinking about the people who knew about Daisy. "I can't think who would have started that rumor."

Her eyes darted around the room. "Oh! It's my good friend Standish Miles, I must go speak to him."

Standish Miles? At least now Jake knew who had started the rumor. He wandered into the room where the pictures of Violet and Daisy were on display. A few people were standing in front of the first one, but they moved on just in time for him to take their place.

Best Laid Plans

The sight of Violet in her flowered dress reminded him of last night. He could feel the buttons, so aggravatingly small, and just beyond them, the rounded flesh of her . . . *don't go there*. If those thoughts continued, he was going to have to find a potted plant to hide behind.

"Jake?" A pretty young woman headed toward him with a big smile on her face. He hated such moments. Had they met, and he didn't recognize her, or had she only seen his picture on a book jacket?

"I'm sorry, I . . ."

She laughed. "It's me, Carrie."

Did he know more than one Carrie? This woman had a sculpted short hairstyle in a darker shade of blonde than the Carrie he'd taken to Wickham, and she was dressed in a slim skirt and jacket even he recognized as stylish. The main difference, however, was in her demeanor. The old Carrie — for indeed, he now saw this was the same person — had slumped, as though she could shrink and hide. Now her posture was straight and her face was animated.

"Wow, you look great! I mean . . ."

"Don't worry, I know what you mean. I feel great, and it's all thanks to you. And Matt."

"Listen, I'm just going to be blunt here. What's going on between you and my uncle?" He'd hoped the two could help each other, but now he was afraid one of them — or both — would end up getting hurt.

She put her hand on his arm. "Do you mind if we step outside?"

He led her out the back door, and she immediately took a cigarette from her bag and lit it. "It's a terrible habit, I know," she said, seeing him cringe. "Your uncle loathes it, and I'm trying to quit." She inhaled deeply and exhaled away from Jake. "Matt is a wonderful man, but I know you hired me to take care of him. I told him I'd think about dating him when he's better, and he thinks he might be able to find me a job in Wickham."

He nodded. "Thank you. Is your old boyfriend leaving you alone?"

The shadow that crossed her face made her seem more like the old Carrie. "So far. I was afraid to come into the city, but I wanted to see the exhibit after Matt raved about it. After my makeover, he told me no one would recognize me."

"He was right. What did you think of the pictures?"

Her smile chased away the shadow. "The ones of Miss Gallagher and Daisy are so beautiful! Will they be put into a book, like the others?" She stubbed out the cigarette with her sandal.

"I don't think so, but I'm going to be taking more for an advertising campaign, I think." He moved toward the door and held it open for her.

"Oh, that's terrific! But you know, I miss Daisy, and I wish I could convince Miss Gallagher I would never have hurt her. Maybe if you need a babysitter sometime I could come in to the city for a few hours or an evening. Your uncle doesn't need me to be there all the time."

Now that they'd found the wonderful Grace Cornelius, Jake couldn't imagine any situation where they might need another babysitter for Daisy. Even if they did, Violet would never let Carrie near the baby again. But he didn't need to tell her that.

"Thanks, Carrie. If we ever do, I know where to reach you."

Chapter Eleven

Violet removed her cotton robe and handed it to the motherly assistant. She had to fight the urge to cover her breasts with her hands. Although the air-conditioning had been adjusted for her comfort, and she stood within a ring of lights, she shivered and felt her nipples stiffen. She was wearing white cotton bikini underpants; the only covering she'd have above the waist would be Daisy.

The assistant handed her the warm, naked baby, and immediately she saw the cons of infants as fashion — she could conceal one breast at a time, but not both. And Daisy squirmed more than the typical bra or shirt.

The baby grinned impishly and grabbed her mother's nose, squeezing hard. Violet hoped she wouldn't try that trick on her exposed nipple. "Now be a good girl, no peeing on Mommy. Or anything else."

"Don't worry, Miss Gallagher, I'll be standing nearby with towels, and we have extra panties, if necessary."

"Thank you, Maeve. That's if I even go through with this. I'm having serious second thoughts." She was, in fact, calculating whether or not she could afford to break her contract with *bébé*.

The grey-haired woman laughed. "I'm sure it's embarrassing. But nothing will, you know, *show*, in the finished pictures. And your husband is taking them, so that will help. Imagine if you had to pose naked for a total stranger!"

Her husband? Is that what everyone thought? They'd probably been told Jake was Daisy's father, and assumed they were married. Getting naked in front of a stranger would be easier, far easier than getting naked in front of Jake. What had she been thinking when she agreed to this?

The day they met with the team from *bébé*, she'd been informed the marketing plan included showing plenty of soft, well cared-for skin, on both baby and mother.

"It will be very tasteful," they'd told her, and she'd thought more about the finished product — and making an appointment at the spa for some skin treatments and a pedicure — than the actual photo shoot. Jake, after all, had seemed unconcerned, nodding and making sketches and notes during the meeting. When their eyes met, he gave her a reassuring smile.

He'd treated her like a model, which is all she was to him, really. Well, that and the mother of his child. But it had been almost two weeks since their adolescent grope session, and nothing had been said about it. They'd been careful to keep a certain distance between them. Perhaps it was simply disinterest on Jake's part, or the fact that he had another woman in his life, one he cold take to a motel where there'd be no interruptions from baby monitors. In any case, what was she worried about? It was Jake who'd be getting an eyeful of her assets, and if it didn't bother him, there was no reason for it to bother her.

"You can let him know we're ready, Maeve."

*

Jake was an artist, first and foremost. He had photographed nude models, many of them as attractive as Violet, many times in his career. So when the people from *bébé* had presented their ideas, he'd been totally onboard. In fact, it was exactly how he'd wanted to pose Violet and Daisy the first time he photographed them — skin-to-skin, natural and unfettered. Violet had demurred, and he'd known then it was just as well.

All those weeks ago she'd been too uptight for the idea to work; she hadn't even known how to play with Daisy, really. But she'd loosened up, and he liked to think he had helped with that process. That he'd been able to do something for her, even if she was completely unaware of it.

Now he was confident she could pose for the photos, and *bébé* would have its ad campaign showing a real mother and baby who used their products, both with healthy, radiant skin and hair. Yes, Violet would be naked, or nearly, but he was a professional. He was like a doctor, really, when it came to the human body.

When he received word she was ready, he walked into the studio where she stood under the lights, holding Daisy against her chest. The baby saw him and arched toward him, exposing much of her mother's breasts. He observed them from his objective, professional viewpoint. They had the slight drop you would expect after a woman had given birth and nursed a baby, but were still exquisite. Round, full, and as he knew from the night he and Violet had fallen asleep together on the sofa, still very firm.

Suddenly aware he'd slipped out of professional mode, he raised his eyes to her face. Color bloomed in her cheeks. She was an artistic vision with her peachy skin, glossy dark hair and sea-blue eyes — but he knew he wasn't being objective anymore.

He took a deep breath to settle himself. "Are you warm enough?"

"I think you've already determined that."

Ouch. "I'm sorry. I didn't mean to make you uncomfortable." Did she think he could take photographs without looking at her? But he knew they needed the camera between them, to hide his eyes and give her the illusion of privacy. He moved toward his equipment and began to make adjustments.

"We'll start with the light background, your skin and hair contrast with it beautifully. Lie down on the platform as though you were on your bed at home. I want you on your side, propped up with your left arm, with Daisy sitting in front of you so you're both facing me. Put your right arm around her belly."

He turned to Maeve. "Make sure as much of Violet is showing as possible, but nothing that shouldn't be." He and Violet had agreed the female assistant would help with the necessary physical adjustments. Now that he saw how easy it was for him to forget this was work, he was glad.

The older woman helped Violet with the pose while a make-up assistant fluffed up her hair. Working with an infant could be difficult, Jake knew, but as soon as the two women stepped out of the frame, Daisy saw her daddy and her face lit up with a huge smile. He started snapping pictures, knowing he had to work quickly.

Before long he slipped into a state of flow, where the work was as natural as breathing, and he lost all sense of time passing. Violet seemed to be right there with him. She lost her self-consciousness and moved easily from pose to pose, matching her reactions to Daisy's. He couldn't stop smiling at what he was seeing through the lens of his camera. Not a woman he wanted to ravage, although she was that; but a woman who had been transformed by motherhood, who had learned to give and nurture. And she was not just any mother, but the mother of *his* perfect child.

A perfect child who had no smiles left to give. Jake checked his watch and was amazed to see thirty minutes had passed. He was sweating in the warm studio and felt like he'd just hiked up a mountain.

"You two are real troopers. I've seen professional models who wore out faster than this. Let's wrap up for the day."

Violet swung around on the padded platform so her back was to him before exchanging the baby for her robe. Although he'd seen her from this angle through the camera, he was seeing her now through the eyes of a man, not a photographer. When she lifted her hair from her neck to cool it, the entire elegant length of her sinuous back was exposed. He imagined placing his tongue at the base of her neck and licking his way down until he reached the tantalizing cleft between those cheeks.

"You're a lucky man, Mr. Macintyre." He forced himself to turn his head and smile at the assistant who had interrupted his reverie. "Your wife is a lovely woman, and such a nice person, too. She brought pastries for the crew this morning."

His *wife*? When he returned his gaze to Violet, she was tying the sash on her robe. Like Daisy, she seemed to have run out of smiles. She'd gotten home from work after midnight, and was up with Daisy at seven, so he marveled at the energy she'd put into the shoot.

In fact, she was a marvel. When he'd believed she'd used him to get pregnant, or even that she'd just decided he didn't need to know his DNA was being passed on, he'd wanted to wring her delicate neck. But he'd had time to think about what it must have been like for her to discover she was pregnant.

He knew by now that Violet was a woman who slept with her day-planner by her bed, and never left the house without a list of errands. He'd seen her add something she'd already done to her to-do list just so she could check it off. She even worked in a business where everything was carefully timed and scripted, and he had no doubt she'd had a timetable for life's major events, like marriage and motherhood. But she'd gone ahead and had the unscheduled baby, even though she knew few people in her new city. Even though the baby's father was on the other side of the world and totally inaccessible even if, by some chance, he'd wanted to be a father.

If she'd tracked him down a year ago, would he have come running back to the States at the news of his impending fatherhood? He recalled the adventures he'd had — which ones would he have been willing to miss so he could carry gifts home from a baby shower? No, Violet had been right to handle things the way she did. He was smitten with Daisy now, and he'd try not to let her down. He might have become a father by accident, but Jake Macintyre wasn't husband material. That was one accident he could prevent.

When he raised his eyes from the equipment he was packing

up, Maeve was standing in front of him. "Your wife and daughter are waiting to say goodbye."

"Miss Gallagher is not my wife."

The woman appeared startled, then focused her eyes on something — or someone — over his shoulder. He followed her gaze, and saw Violet standing in the doorway with Daisy. She turned and went out the door without a word.

*

An hour later, Jake was pulling camping gear out of Jamie's guestroom closet when he heard his brother's footsteps in the hall. He swore to himself, and considered jumping into the closet and pulling everything in after him. He'd been hoping to make a fast and clean getaway.

"Time to get out of Dodge?"

Too late. "I'm going to camp in the mountains for the weekend. I just need some fresh air and a break from the city." He didn't bother telling Jamie he wasn't trying to escape from anything; his brother knew him too well.

"Excellent idea. A little fishing, some canned beans heated over the campfire. Hand me my backpack, and I'll be ready in twenty minutes."

Jake didn't bother to stifle his groan.

Jamie put his hands on his hips. "Hey, you store your gear at my place, this is the price you pay. Besides, we haven't camped together in years. Would it be so awful?"

He had to admit if he couldn't be alone, his brother was the only person he'd want sharing his tent. Although his sleeping bag was another matter altogether, and he imagined slipping into his down cocoon with Violet. Then he reminded himself he'd be too tired to do anything but sleep after completing the fifty-item checklist she'd insist upon for their safety.

"You can come. Just don't talk too much."

An hour later they were on the highway heading toward the Berkshires. With his brother along, there was too much gear to fit into his rental car, so Jamie was piloting his luxury SUV while Jake pondered where his plan to get away and rough it had gone wrong.

He flipped open his cell phone and called Violet. As he'd hoped, it went to voice mail. She was probably screening and didn't want to talk to him. He left a brief message telling her where he was going.

"I won't have my phone on during the day, but I'll check for messages before I turn in for the night." He flipped it shut and tucked it into his knapsack on the seat behind him.

"You didn't even tell her you were going?"

Jake didn't like what the question implied. "I didn't have to. We're not married."

His brother laughed so hard he didn't hear the instructions coming from the GPS system. "And not likely to be!"

"Look who's talking." He'd been cooped up with his brother for only twenty minutes, and already Jake felt like he was eleven years old again. "You were supposed to turn left back there."

It wasn't until they were bedded down for the night, inches apart in the tent, that Jake brought up the subject again. "Have you ever thought about it? Why neither of us seems able to settle down with one woman?"

He heard his brother inhale deeply before he spoke. "I settle down with one woman all the time."

"Maybe I need to define 'settle down' for you, bro."

Jamie laughed softly. "I know, I know. My therapist — yes, I've had therapy, don't make fun of me or I'll pound you — says I never had a happy marriage model to learn from. My memories of Mom and Dad together are hazy, at best, and my memories of Mom's second marriage are all too clear. I'd say I'm following the model set by Uncle Matt."

"Uncle Matt says he's going to marry Carrie. Do you think he's serious?" Jake struggled to get comfortable on the hard ground and wished he hadn't turned down his brother's offer of an air mattress. A couple months of memory foam mattresses, and he was spoiled.

"I think he's just intrigued because she won't sleep with him. Matt acquired confirmed bachelor status years ago."

His brother seemed so sure of everything. He remembered how Jamie had laughed earlier at the idea of Jake ever getting married. Was he already as set in his ways as his uncle?

"So your therapist thinks we'll never settle down just because we can't remember our parents having a happy marriage?"

There was such a long silence his brother might have fallen asleep.

"Even if you could get past that, you couldn't stay in one place long enough for it to happen. You were so young you don't even remember, but after Dad died you wandered off so often, Mom had to start tying you up."

It was true he didn't remember, but every time Jake heard the story his heart raced. He had a terrible fear of small spaces and being confined, but one fear surpassed it by far.

"When she got sick . . ." his brother's voice tapered off without finishing the thought.

Jake's conscience prickled. "I wasn't around much and left you with that burden, Jamie. You know I'm sorry, don't you?"

Again there was a heavy silence, and Jake was glad they were having this conversation in the dark.

"I never blamed you for that, you were just a kid. But in a way, I feel sorry for you. I spent a lot of time with Mom, reading to her from those travel books she loved about all the places she wanted to see, and I really got to know her. You missed out on something special."

Jake remembered listening outside his mother's bedroom door to Jamie promising he'd take her someday to all the exotic places she wanted to see, a promise all three of them knew was a lie.

They'd made lists Jake would find in the kitchen in the morning. The Great Wall. The Pyramids. The Eiffel Tower. Jake had been to all of them.

"She was a wonderful woman." His brother's voice was fading out. "I haven't found another one who could compare to her."

Jake thought maybe he had.

*

Although he'd set it to vibrate, Jamie never turned his phone off the whole weekend, which caused Jake a lot of confusion. He'd think his brother was talking to him, when he was actually talking to a client. When he checked his messages again before starting up the SUV on Sunday, it reminded Jake he should check back in with civilization as well.

The only message he had was from Grace Cornelius, telling him she had a family emergency and wouldn't be able to watch Daisy on Monday, and should she give Violet a call too?

He hit redial and told Grace he'd let Violet know, even as he searched his mind for a solution. He'd asked Grace to sit so he could go to the television studio and be interviewed by Violet for her show. It was important to her, and he hated to cancel at the last minute.

"Who can I get to watch Daisy tomorrow?" he said out loud to himself.

"Don't look at me, I'd rather fight a black bear for my picnic basket." His brother smiled as they bumped their way out of the State Park.

"Carrie's trustworthy now, don't you think? Violet doesn't have to know."

"If she finds out, *you'd* be better off fighting with the black bear."

"True enough." But he dialed his Uncle Matt's number anyway.

*

Violet hadn't done an in-depth interview since leaving Wickham, and she was nervous. It didn't help that she was interviewing Jake. But he'd made it clear at the photo session on Friday that what they had was a professional relationship; now she'd be the one in charge, doing her job. And it was her job to get Jake to reveal something about himself, whether she was personally interested in his revelation or not.

She scanned her list of prepared questions, and starred the ones she considered most important. During the interview she might follow an intriguing tangent, but having the list would give her a base to return to. Her brother could tease her about her lack of spontaneity, but a large portion of what she did was unscripted. Once she had established a rapport with her subject, the skill came naturally.

But would it happen with Jake?

He'd seemed nervous when he arrived at the studio, and distracted, even evasive, when she asked him how Daisy's day was going. Maybe she'd make a quick call to Grace, just to ease her mind.

She was reaching for the phone when someone knocked on her dressing room door. "They're ready to do your make-up, Miss Gallagher."

"Coming." She rose quickly to her feet. It was rude to keep people waiting, and she was certain Daisy was just fine.

*

"This time I get to turn the cameras on you." Violet and Jake sat facing each other in director's chairs on one of the studio sets. "At least when you work with me, you get to wear clothes."

In his well-worn jeans, scuffed boots, white T-shirt and khaki jacket, he could be the leading man in an adventure movie, the hero who would bring back the treasure — and the girl. All that was missing was a pith helmet, but it would be a shame to cover up his curly golden hair.

He grinned. "Good, because my skin isn't as smooth as yours." Violet's shoulders tensed; she didn't want to begin on a personal note. Best to just keep moving instead of saying anything.

"I'll introduce you and talk about your work, and then we'll just chat. I might ask you something that turns out not to be relevant, and take it out later. If you're ready, we'll start the cameras."

He swallowed hard, which told her he was nervous. "You're the boss."

She nodded to the cameraman, then turned back to Jake. After a short intro and welcome, she began with the first question on the list.

"Jake, you've had a long career for such a young man. Can you tell me how you got started in photography? Did you have a formal education, or are you self-taught?"

"Some of both." He shifted in the tall chair, but his eyes never left her face. "My father died when I was six, and his last gift to me was the Kodak Instamatic camera I'd asked Santa Claus to bring me for Christmas. Of course I was much too young for it, so my mother put it away until I was a few years older. I'd never get anything else from him, so I wanted to make it last a lifetime, so to speak. I snapped pictures everywhere I went, and got a paper route so I'd have money for film. Later, when I went to college, I majored in journalism but took a few photography courses."

His father died when he was only six? Although her smile didn't waver, Violet prickled with embarrassment over all the whining she'd done about her father's neglect. At least he'd been alive.

"How did your father die?" This was one of those tangents; she didn't expect to use the answer in the finished interview.

A cloud passed over his eyes and his smile vanished. "An industrial accident."

She sensed she would get nothing more from him on that subject, and shifted gears.

"You said you studied journalism. Were you a writer before you were a photographer?"

The smile came back. "Yes, but not for long. I was an intern for a camping magazine when I got caught borrowing their darkroom to develop my pictures. Luckily for me, my boss liked my work enough to give me an assignment. He actually called it 'my work,' which was a defining moment for me. Then he sent me to the Acadia National Park in Maine to do a story on solo wilderness camping. You can't go solo and bring a photographer, so I did it all."

"Do you remember the amount of your first check?"

"Five hundred dollars. It was the first time I'd ever been paid to do what I loved best, and I resolved right then it wouldn't be the last."

Violet, preoccupied with scanning her question list, almost missed the ambiguity in his answer. "You said you were paid to do what you loved best. Did you mean taking pictures, or camping in the wilderness?"

His eyebrows shot up. "Well, not camping, exactly. Going someplace I'd never been. Having adventures."

She nodded; it was what she'd suspected he meant. "Because your father died when you were so young, you probably didn't have much opportunity to travel before you became an adult."

His sudden laughter surprised her. "I did a lot of traveling, starting when I was six. I'd go off on foot or on my bike and end up in some neighborhood I'd never been before. My mother had to come with the car to retrieve me on more than one occasion."

Violet understood then just how firmly his wanderlust was entrenched. Even if he wanted to stay in one place, he probably couldn't do it.

She moved on to the next question on her list, the one she liked the least because it was going to affect her life too. Not that she wanted or needed Jake around, but the routine they'd established was working well. She'd been told she didn't handle transitions well and knew it was true.

"Your books have been very successful. I understand you recently returned from Russia and Tibet, and will have two books coming out next year. Where are you heading next?"

He opened his mouth, then closed it again. He bit his lip, frowning in concentration, and finally laughed. "I guess we'll have to tape this part over, because I've forgotten! I'll have to call Millie and ask her, but she'll probably kill me."

"You're going to Peru," she reminded him, having gotten the information from his agent when she prepared for the interview.

"Oh, right." He grinned. "I should have known you'd do your homework."

She repeated the question, and he told her about his plans to explore the Incan culture, growing more animated as he talked. She didn't know what it meant that he had forgotten his destination, but she had no doubt he was eager to go.

"I just have one more question. You have a reputation as a man's man, someone who will go anywhere and do anything. I wondered if you have a phobia, one thing that really scares you." She expected him to say no, or reply with a joke. Once again, he surprised her.

"Yes, I do. Fire."

Chapter Twelve

Jake had been about to tell Violet — and the Boston viewers — about his fear of being confined. That would have been bad enough, but at least it would make sense to people. The guy camps by himself in the wilderness, okay, because he's claustrophobic and likes a lot of space. Why, then, had he said fire? It would make people wonder what had happened to him, Violet included. Nosy types might even ask him to explain. In fact, that would probably be her next question.

He cleared his throat. "Umm, could I ask you not to use that part? We can do it over if you want. As it turns out, I have a lot of phobias." He flashed what he hoped was a charming smile, showing lots of teeth. He'd given Violet veto power over the photographs he took of her, but she'd made no similar offer. He was forced to throw himself on her mercy.

To his surprise, she let the issue drop. "I think we have enough without it. It has to be cut down to ten minutes anyway." She stood up and held out her hand the way she might to any interviewee. There was no chance Violet's staff was going to suspect they had a personal relationship. Her hand was warm and dry, but his palm was sweaty.

"Thanks for giving me your time, Jake. I think it's going to be a great segment."

He hoped so, given the risk he'd taken asking Carrie to sit for Daisy. "It was my pleasure."

Violet walked away to confer with her producer, leaving Jake feeling abandoned. He'd considered asking her to go to dinner with him between newscasts, but it was probably best he get back home — to Violet's, rather — and relieve Carrie. The less time she spent with Daisy, the less chance Violet would find out what he'd done.

Everything was fine back at the townhouse. Daisy was all smiles, and so was Carrie. She thanked him effusively for giving her a chance to make amends, and refused his offer of payment before taking off in his uncle's truck. So he was feeling smug when Violet walked in at midnight carrying a chilled bottle of champagne.

"It was a gift from my producer. Will you join me in a celebration?"

"Of course. But what are we celebrating?" He worked on removing the cork while she went to the cabinet for the fluted glasses.

"He liked the segment and wants me to do more. In fact, we talked about the possibility of my own weekly program."

"Would you still anchor the news?" The cork came out with a subdued pop — he didn't want to wake Daisy — and he filled their glasses.

Violet's smile was radiant. "No, that's the best part! My hours would be more flexible, and I could spend a lot more time with Daisy."

"Won't you miss it?"

She sat down next to him on the sofa and sipped her wine before answering. He was reminded of her farewell party in Wickham, although she hadn't been sipping that night. She'd drained her glass in two swallows and then he'd handed her another. Tonight he'd make sure she either stayed sober, went to bed alone, or both. As tempting as it was to let history repeat itself, he believed in learning the lessons history presented.

"I realized when I was interviewing you today just how bored I am with anchoring the news. You're so passionate about what you do. Even a stick-in-the-mud like me could see the attraction of traveling and creating art." She set her glass on the table and leaned back against the cushions.

"I'm very fortunate to be able to do what I love. My mother never got to travel, although it was her greatest wish. Well, second greatest. I know wanting me and Jamie to turn out well was number one." He'd wished his mother could have seen the turnout at the gallery for his exhibit; she'd have been amazed at far he'd come since the day she handed him the Instamatic.

"I don't know Jamie very well, but I'm sure she'd be proud of the way you turned out."

"Thank you. But you must be tired. I've already bored you with my life story enough for one day."

She smiled and shook her head. "I'm wide awake. I'd like to hear more about your mother."

"The first pictures I took, on my travels around the neighborhood, were for her. And the pictures I take now, in all the exotic places she never got to go, they're for her too." He emptied his wine glass and set it on the coffee table next to Violet's full one. He was still sitting on the edge of the sofa when he felt her shift forward and place her hand on his forearm.

"Jake, will you tell me why you're afraid of fire? I've always wondered how you got the scar on your back. You were burned, weren't you?"

In over twenty years, he had never told anyone how he got the scar — Jamie and his uncle were the only living people who knew. Ellsworth, the slimy scumbag, had finally died last year. Of an especially nasty type of cancer, he'd heard, which made him believe in divine retribution, or karma, depending on which hemisphere he was standing in when he thought about it. He took a deep breath and began to tell his story for the first time.

"My mother's second husband was an abusive alcoholic. One night, after he was done slapping her around, he passed out on the sofa with a lit cigarette in his hand. It dropped to the carpet, and smoldered there for hours."

He took a deep breath, and she squeezed his arm in encouragement. "I woke up and went down to the kitchen for a glass of water. I discovered the fire, which by then was making its way up the end of the sofa and the pillow the creep was snoring on. I yelled for Jamie and my mother to get out while they could still get to the front door, and I had every intention of following right behind them. Ellsworth was going to roast in hell anyway, I figured he might as well get a head start."

"How old were you?"

"Twelve. But I was a very old twelve." He smiled at her, and she nodded that she understood.

"Did your stepfather die in the fire?"

Jake's heart raced. Just as he had that night, he saw Ellsworth wake with a snort and turn his head jerkily from side to side, disoriented and confused. When Jake passed him he accidentally made eye contact with the man, and saw the dawning panic in his eyes.

"George!" his mother screamed as she came down the stairs.

"Ma, keep moving," Jamie yelled back. "You have to go next door and call the fire department. We'll get him out, don't worry."

Jake, rooted to the spot next to the now-flaming couch, watched his mother run out the door through the growing haze of the smoke. Jamie, standing near the door, shook his head, and gestured with his hand for him to come. But Jake turned back again to Ellsworth, who was yelling and brushing at his clothes, which were now on fire.

"Jake, leave him! Save yourself!"

Ignoring his brother, he ran upstairs and pulled the blanket from his bed. With smoke beginning to burn in his lungs, he tried to take shallow breaths as he returned to the living room and threw the cover over Ellsworth, wrapping him in it as best he could to smother the fire. He wanted only to get out, to run and run and never stop, but he pulled on the older man's big legs with his twelve-year-old arms.

"Jamie, help me pull him out!"

Then his brother was at his side, but instead of helping him drag Ellsworth off the couch, he grabbed a throw pillow and beat at Jamie's back with it. "Your shirt's on fire! We have to get out, now!"

Hearing sirens, he'd let his brother pull him by the arm and out of the smoke-filled house.

By the time he finished his story, Violet had moved closer. Her arm was now around his back. "Did he live?"

He ran a shaking hand through his short curls. "Yes."

"Was he grateful to you for saving his life? Did he treat your mother — and you and Jamie — better after the fire?"

She sounded so hopeful, he wished he could give the story a happy ending. "He was scarred and deformed and in pain the rest of his life. Somehow he managed to blame us. He was more abusive, not less."

Violet clung to him so tightly her hand dug into his side. "Did your mother ever get away from him?"

This time he could give her the answer she wanted. "Yes. She got cancer, and he took off. He left me and Jamie to take care of our dying mother, and it was a blessed relief for all of us."

When she said nothing more, he finally turned his head. Her blue eyes swam with tears. He raised a finger to her cheek and caught one as it dropped, then touched it to his tongue and tasted its salt. Violet took hold of his finger and pulled it away, replacing it with her lips. Instead of her tears, he savored the sweet-salty flavor of her mouth.

Although he longed to take her in his arms, to let her kisses and caresses erase the ugly memories, he held back. He didn't want her to make love to him out of pity; that would be even worse than the first time, when she'd done it under false pretences. There could be no more misunderstandings between them.

Her kisses grew more intense, and she pressed herself against him while clutching the back of his head. When he still failed to respond, she groaned in frustration and pulled back to peer into his eyes again. "Is it because you have another woman?"

He shook his head. "No. I know what you thought, but I can explain about the hotel receipt. And I will, but not tonight." Telling her about Carrie might be harder than telling the story about the fire, because Violet was single-minded when it came to keeping the nanny away from Daisy. But at least now she would understand why he'd felt he had to help Carrie, who was a victim of abuse like his mother.

"Then I want to make love to you. Don't you want that too?"

He grasped her hands, the only part of her he could safely touch. "More than anything. I've wanted it every day since I came home, even the day I came here and yelled at your brother and threatened to get a lawyer. And I wanted it before that, when I was away. The memory of our one night together has haunted me for a year."

"Then why are you resisting?"

"Because now I know you want more than a fling, and I can't give it to you. You deserve more than I can offer."

She guided his hands inside the jacket she'd worn to work, and he was helpless to resist the opportunity to cup her warm breasts in his hands once more. "Violet," he groaned.

Her breath was warm against his ear when she whispered her response. "I don't know what I deserve, but I know what I want. Another night with you. Tonight."

"It isn't because you feel sorry for me after I told you my sad story, is it?"

The sound she made was a cross between a groan and a laugh. "Oh, Jake, I could never feel sorry for you."

Reassured — or maybe just too desperate with desire not to believe her — he undid the three large buttons on her jacket and slipped it off her shoulders, then reached behind her and unhooked her bra. Just when it would have fallen free, she pinned it back in place with both hands.

"Oh, there's something I forgot."

It was his turn to groan. "What?"

"I had my lawyer write up a contract. It spells out what will happen in the case of accidental pregnancy." Her eyes danced with mischief.

"Do you have fresh condoms?" he asked her.

"Yes. Well, fresher than the last time, anyway. But they're completely untested."

"Then I'm willing to take my chances. I thrive on danger."

He pulled her hands away. When the lacy bra fell, revealing her beautiful breasts once again, he took first one rosy nipple and then the other into his mouth. He planned to taste every inch of her and couldn't do so in such cramped quarters, so he forced himself to stand and hold out his hand to her.

"Would you care to join me in my dangerous venture?"

"Will there be treasure at the end?"

He pulled her up and into his arms, unable to wait until they reached the bedroom to kiss her again. "I've already found the treasure."

*

Jake held out his hand to her, and Violet let him lead her up the stairs. She'd only had a few mouthfuls of her wine, and knew she was in complete control of her decision-making capabilities. In fact, she'd made up her mind hours ago that the night would end this way; when her producer presented her with the chilled champagne she'd considered the reminder of that fateful night last summer a sign.

In her inebriated and vulnerable state, she'd thought the night she met him that Jake was someone she could fall in love with. After the interview today, she knew she already had. She also knew exactly what loving Jake would entail.

Although she was anxious to get to the bedroom, her legs weak with her need and desire, almost comically so, she pulled her hand from Jake's as they passed the nursery.

"Just let me take a second to check on Daisy," she whispered.

"Okay," he hissed back, "but for God's sake, don't wake her up."

As she stood by the crib, reassured by the rise and fall of the baby's ribcage in the glow from the nightlight, she sensed rather than heard Jake enter the room behind her. He slipped his arm around her waist and gazed down at the sleeping infant. When he raised his head and their eyes met, she knew their shared bond could never be broken, no matter how much time and distance came between them.

It was her turn to take his hand and lead him from the room.

Violet already knew how exciting it was to make love to a handsome stranger, at least when the stranger was Jake. Tonight she was discovering love was an even more powerful aphrodisiac, and the familiarity of his handsome face and well-put-together body didn't make it any less thrilling.

They stopped when they reached the foot of the bed to kiss and embrace, and Jake ran his hands over her breasts, brushing each nipple in slow circles. Craving the feel of his hard chest against her breasts, she pushed his tee-shirt up as high as it would go.

He groaned. "I want to take this slow." He pressed his lips against hers and then worked his tongue inside her mouth, exploring it thoroughly. "But I also want to throw you down on the bed, push this skirt up to your waist, and have you right now. I might not even bother to remove your panties."

As he spoke, he slid his hands up her thighs inside the skirt, and by the time he said "panties" his fingers had pushed inside the thin fabric and were caressing her most sensitive places. The sensation was both ecstatic and unbearable at the same time.

"That would be a shame." Her breath caught in her throat.

"Yes, it would." His sigh was warm against her ear. "How would I know if you were ready for me?" His finger parted her lips and slid into the wetness it found there.

She couldn't stand it any longer. "Let me help by taking off this skirt."

Gradually they released their hold on each other so she could undo the back zipper and step out of her skirt. She slipped off her sandals as well, blessing the new fashion trend allowing her to skip pantyhose in the summer.

Meanwhile, Jake tore off his clothes. By the time he got down to his white boxers, she couldn't resist slipping her hands inside the elastic and sliding them down, sinking to her knees as she did so. Remembering how he'd worked her panties down so slowly the first time they were together, and then run his tongue over the all the deliciously sensitive nerve endings they'd been covering, she did the same to him now. After his erection was thoroughly wet and his legs were so weak he had to sink back against the bed, she covered it with quick, tiny kisses.

He slipped both hands under her arms and pulled her onto the bed with him. "I'm taking that as a vote against going slow." His voice was husky as she pressed herself against the length of his body, her bikini underpants the only thing between them now. He bent over her, licked her belly, and continued down, his tongue touching her most sensitive spot, but through the silky fabric.

"Oh, just rip them off!"

He laughed and continued to tease her.

"I'm not kidding. I haven't had sex in over a year, and I can't wait any longer."

He worked the panties down her legs so she could push them off completely with her feet, and then slid back up so they were face-to-face again. "Stop complaining, woman. You're not the only one."

Was he telling her he hadn't made love to anyone else since the night Daisy was conceived? She held herself away from him so she could gaze into his amber eyes. "You haven't been with anyone else? Why not?"

She felt him shrug under her hands. "I wasn't sure why, until just this minute. I thought I'd lost my sex drive."

"Which seems just fine now," she said, after reaching down to check and giving his rock-hard erection a few tender strokes. The drops of liquid at the tip told her she'd have to search the nightstand for the condoms before they went much further. "Then why?"

He kissed her again before replying, a kiss that made her forget the question, and even her name. "You spoiled me for anyone else. I guess that's what love does."

Her eyes filled with tears. Instead of answering, she rolled away to retrieve a silver packet from the drawer and handed it to him. "I think we've both waited long enough."

Jake ripped open the packet and rolled onto his back, pulling her on top of him seconds later. It had always made Violet self-conscious to be on top, but in the moonlight filtering through the blinds, Jake smiled at her like she was the world's greatest work of art. Then, just as she had when he'd observed her through his camera lens, she forgot her body, forgot everything now but how good it felt to have Jake inside her, filling her body and soul. With their eyes locked, she rocked them both to a shuddering and seemingly endless climax.

"I love you," she said as she collapsed against him.

*

When Violet woke, the first thing she did was stretch out her arm in search of Jake. But just like the last time she'd shared her bed with him, she was alone, and the sheets on the other side of the bed were cool. There was no shower running, but when she grabbed a robe and headed down the hall, she heard Daisy laughing.

Jake was holding her in the glider, an empty bottle on the table beside him. He held a burp cloth over his eyes and let it fall. "Peekaboo!" The baby convulsed with giggles.

Feeling ready to laugh herself, with relief that she'd found him and delight at the father-daughter bonding, she stood behind the chair and rested her chin on Jake's curly hair. She placed her hands on his shoulders and kneaded, unable to resist touching him. Was it her imagination, or did his shoulders stiffen instead of relaxing?

"Good morning," she said, moving in front of him so she could see his face. He was already showered and dressed in clean clothes. Instead of snuggling in her bed in morning-after contentment, and possibly making love again, he'd been up even before the baby.

His only response was a smile that never reached his eyes.

Daisy pulled herself to a half-sitting position and reached out to her mother. Violet took her from Jake. "Thanks for getting up with her."

"I figured you needed your sleep."

His remark should have been followed by a shared, suggestive smile, but it was not. Violet wanted to cry. She'd known this would happen, but she'd thought they could have a month together first. Why had she told him she loved him? He'd used the word first, and she felt like she'd been tricked.

"I'd like to take Daisy to the park this morning after breakfast. Would you like to come with us?" His eyes were sad, his smile still in hiding.

She handed Daisy back to him. "Give me an hour to get ready." But she knew she would never be ready for what he was going to say to her.

*

"We made a mistake."

Daisy had fallen asleep in her stroller, and the moment she'd dreaded was here. Jake sat about a foot away from her on the park bench, and she longed to close the gap between them. Instead she angled herself so he would have to see her face when he lied to her — and to himself.

"I told you I knew what I was doing. I wanted to make love last night."

"And what do you want now?" He crossed his arms, and she felt like yanking them away from his chest.

What did she want? If she were honest, she would have to say she wanted him to stop traveling, move into her townhouse and be her lover and partner 24/7. Marriage would be nice, too. While she was at it, she could also put in a request for world peace and an end to global warming.

She settled for something less than honest. "Whatever you can give us, Jake."

The corner of his lip turned down in a skeptical grimace. "You say that now, but when all I can give you is frustration, it won't be good enough."

"It seems like last night was the end of a year of frustration, for both of us."

Jake uncrossed his arms and pulled Violet into his arms. She nestled her face against his chest, inhaling his scent like it was essential to life.

"I realized I'm falling in love with you. That could lead to some lonely nights in Chile this winter."

"Peru."

"Right. Not to mention the lonely nights for you, here in Boston. I want you to go on with your life. You were always waiting for your father when you were a child, and I refuse to be another man who lets you down."

Her tears soaked into his shirt. "What happens now?"

"I'm going to move back in with Jamie. I'll spend as much time with Daisy as I can, but I think we should start breaking in a new nanny." His arms tightened around her, even as he was telling her he wanted to put more distance between them.

Daisy woke with a start, and began to cry when she didn't immediately see her parents. Jake let Violet go and reached for the baby instead. "Daddy's right here, don't cry."

Once he had her on his lap, he turned back to Violet. "I'm not going to abandon Daisy. You and I may not be lovers, but I'm going to be part of your life for a long, long time."

Yes, that would be *much* less frustrating.

Chapter Thirteen

When Jake emerged from the Callahan Tunnel and saw the billboard, he was so stunned by the sight of Violet, thirty feet of reclining maternal splendor — not to mention that, except for the parts Daisy covered up, she was *nude* — he rear-ended a Lexus.

He followed the other driver to the shoulder, where he and Jamie hopped out of his rented car. They gaped at the image together in something like reverence.

"I suppose this means I'm going to miss my flight," his brother grumbled, but good-naturedly.

The driver of the Lexus, who'd been examining his bumper, huffed over to them. Seeing them stare, he followed their gaze to the billboard, shading his eyes from the glare of the setting sun reflected in the windows above it. "That's why you hit me? What, you've never seen a naked woman before?"

Jake took a fast step toward the guy — how dare he talk about Violet? In fact, he didn't even like him looking at her. Jamie grabbed his arm and yanked him to a stop. "Let me handle this," he hissed in his ear.

Jamie slapped the other driver on the back. "Nice car. It's almost indestructible, right? I'll bet we didn't even leave a mark on it with this flimsy piece of junk my brother's driving." He pulled out a business card and handed it to the irate man as he led him back over to the Lexus.

They stooped down in unison, and Jake watched his brother run his hand over the car's bumper while the owner gestured and jabbered. In thirty minutes the two of them would probably be having a drink at the airport bar and sharing stock tips. Meanwhile, he'd be headed back to the city, where he'd arrive at Violet's just in time to put Daisy to bed. Too late, actually, but he'd phoned Grace this afternoon and asked her to keep the baby up until he arrived.

He returned his gaze to the billboard and the gigantic smiling face of his baby girl. She'd been four months old then, able to roll over, reach for things, and hold her head at a full ninety-degree angle, the way she was in the picture. Now, only a few weeks later, she could sit by herself, hunched over her rolls of baby fat like a miniature Buddha. The fuzzy hair like duck down she had in the picture had grown into soft curls, another way she resembled him, and she was cutting her first tooth.

In a month he would be gone. In thirteen months, when he came back, she'd be walking and saying words. "Daddy" wouldn't be one of them.

"Let's go," Jamie called to him as he climbed back in the car.

"No police report?" He started the car and waited for the Lexus to pull back into traffic before entering the stream of cars headed for Logan.

His brother laughed. "He thought a thousand dollars would be enough to get his invisible scratch rubbed out. No need to get the police and insurance companies involved."

"That's blackmail."

"I'll pay the guy. It's worth it to me to make this flight tonight. Thanks again for the ride, by the way. I assume you didn't know your child and her mother were already towering above the streets of Boston."

Jake stared again at the billboard as they passed beneath it, then shook his head. "Millie said they were going to rush the ad campaign. Now the only way I can avoid seeing Violet everywhere is to leave the country."

Leave the country. His editor could finish the book without him. If he set the process in motion today, he could be in Peru in five days, a week at the most. Twice he'd forgotten his destination, and now he knew why — he hated the idea of going, of missing

Daisy's milestones. Of having her forget him. He could only hope the old excitement would come back once he got there and immersed himself in his work. After all, hadn't that always been the balm for him in the past when he was hurting?

"You'll be out of here soon enough. I know you're going to miss her. Miss both of them."

How could he explain to his brother that he already missed Violet? He hadn't told him the real reason he'd moved back to the penthouse three weeks ago, just that he and Violet had agreed it would be best if they put some distance between them. They had phased Grace Cornelius in as Daisy's new nanny, and, although he tried to spend some time with the baby every day, he hadn't seen or even spoken to Violet in a week.

Except in his dreams. Waking up hot, sweaty, and hard had become a regular occurrence, one he hoped would cease once he put a continent between them — which he planned to do just as soon as possible. He'd call Violet tomorrow and let her know he was changing his plans. He knew he'd hurt her by moving out, now he just wanted to minimize the damage. To both of them.

While Jamie retrieved his bag from the trunk of the car, Jake took out his cell phone. It was turned off, as usual — he'd just never gotten in the habit of using it, and wouldn't use it at all once he was back at work. As always, he'd carry nothing but his camera. That had never been a concern in the past, because Millie and his publisher were always able to reach him — eventually. But that was before he knew about Daisy. He sighed. One night of sex with Violet sure had complicated his life. The second night? It had nearly destroyed him.

Waving goodbye to Jamie, he punched in Millie's number and left a message telling her to have her assistant move up his travel arrangements. After promising to call her first thing in the morning, he tossed the cell phone onto the dash and drove back toward the city, and Daisy.

He was halfway to Violet's when it rang. It would be Millie, he knew, calling him back to tell him why he couldn't go yet. He reached for it and pressed the green button. "I'm going."

"Jake? Jake, you have to get here as fast as you can!" The caller — not Millie — was sobbing, close to hysteria.

"Who is . . . Grace, is that you?"

"There's a fire. I called 911. They're on the way. But Daisy . . ."

"What about Daisy?" He heard sirens, then yelling. "Grace? Grace, talk to me!" The line went dead.

Minutes later, he stopped his car in the middle of the street in front of Violet's townhouse. He left the door ajar and the engine running, and, with his feet barely touching the ground, he wove his way between fire trucks and leapt over hoses, pushing bystanders and emergency workers out of the way as he ran. Violet's front door had been broken open with an axe, and the firefighters were spraying the foyer — the only route to Daisy's nursery.

"Jake!" He turned his head and saw Grace, limp in the arms of a rescue worker. There was no sign of Daisy.

"Hey! You can't go in there!" A fireman stopped him at the door, or tried to.

A quick punch to the midsection sent the guy reeling just long enough for Jake to bound past him. He pulled his shirt up over his nose, and entered the smoke-filled hallway. The stairs were straight ahead. Daisy's room was at the top, and he reached it in three leaps. Coughing, he burst through the closed door. The smoke hadn't seeped into the room yet, so it was easy to see. But he couldn't believe what he was seeing — Daisy's crib was empty. No baby, no blankets or teddy bear. Nothing. If they'd already gotten her out, where was she? Why hadn't Grace told him?

A fireman tackled him from behind while another rushed past him and grabbed the side of the crib. "Where's the kid? The babysitter said she was in here."

Jake saw red, thought he might be having a stroke but didn't care. "You mean you don't have her? Then where the hell is she?"

"Kelly, get him out of here." The second fireman to enter the room spoke to the one who was holding Jake. "Me and Jenkins will search the rest of the house."

Although he struggled, Jake was no match for Kelly. Seconds later he was outside with Grace, who was now being questioned by a female police officer.

He dropped to his knees in front of her. "Grace, where did you leave Daisy?"

The baffled expression on her face was the most frightening thing he'd ever seen. "I put her to bed. I know you wanted me to wait for you, but she was so cranky. When she had her bottle she fell asleep..."

It took all his willpower not to yell at the woman. She seemed old and frail. Why had they trusted her with the baby? "Grace, she's not in her crib now."

"I don't understand." Her voice was barely audible. "Where else could she be?"

Jake stood up, his body primed for action but with no action to take. He walked back toward the house just as the trio of firemen emerged from the front door. One of them caught the eye of the police officer. He shook his head and raised his empty hands. They hadn't found Daisy.

"Jake? Where's Daisy? Is she all right?" Violet was running toward him.

He pulled her into his arms, but it was like trying to hold a wild bear. The worst part of it was, there was nothing he could say to calm her. "I don't know."

"Sir? Are you the baby's father?" The police officer had to yell to be heard over Violet's screams and sobs. "How old is the baby? Is she walking?"

"No!" he yelled back. "She's only five months old."

"Can you think of any reason someone might have taken her?"

Suddenly Violet became a dead, quiet weight in Jake's arms.

Violet was conscious for several seconds before she dared to open her eyes. She prayed that somehow, when she did, the nightmare would be over and she would be safe in her bed, listening to Daisy's whispery breaths over the baby monitor. However, the hubbub she heard all around her — static-riddled conversation on two-way radios, men shouting, and a woman sobbing — told her what was happening was all too real. When she gave up and forced her eyelids open, they felt like they had weights attached to them.

After a moment she understood she was lying on a gurney inside a brightly lit ambulance, with an I.V. in one arm and a blood pressure cuff inflated on the other. The air whooshed out of the cuff, and the paramedic removed the stethoscope from her ears and looked at her with the kindest eyes she had ever seen. Her sympathetic gaze confirmed Violet was that most tragic of victims, a mother whose child was missing — or dead. Violet, as a newswoman, knew the statistics. If they didn't find Daisy soon, they likely would never find her alive.

"She's awake," the woman said to someone Violet couldn't see. "Should I give her more?"

Violet struggled to make her dry tongue meet the roof of her mouth. "No!" She felt the pressure of someone squeezing her hand.

"Let them help you, sweetheart." It was Jake.

"I need to be awake when . . . when they bring her home." Many times in her career Violet had reported stories of missing children, and interviewed heartbroken mothers. She'd always wondered how the mothers clung so staunchly to the belief that *their* child would be one of the lucky ones. Now she knew — it was impossible to believe anything else.

Jake took her hand in both of his. "We'll find her. I promise." Tears had traced a path through a layer of black soot coating his face.

"You went inside, didn't you? Are you hurt?" She struggled to sit up so she could examine him more closely.

He held up his right hand, which appeared swollen and red. "Only where I connected with the fireman who tried to keep me out."

She remembered the night he'd told her about saving his stepfather from the fire, and the feel of his scar under her hand the night they'd made love. He'd gone into the house despite his well-earned fear of fire, in a futile attempt to retrieve his child. He might not have survived.

"Oh, Jake, Daisy's gone and you could have been killed, and it's all my fault!" The tears came again, and wouldn't stop. Jake stood and put his arms around her where she sat on the gurney, rocking her and making soothing sounds.

When she was worn out, her sobs replaced by hiccupping gasps, he asked her what she'd meant.

"I insisted on doing the ad campaign."

"You think that's why Daisy was kidnapped, if she was?"

"Of course she was kidnapped, Jake, she didn't walk out of the house by herself! I'm sure someone saw her picture and figured they could get money from me." She began to cry again. "And they can, all I have and more. If they'll just give Daisy back unharmed."

"We've called in the FBI, Miss Gallagher." Violet had been unaware the policewoman had climbed into the ambulance with them. "They want to know where they can meet with you."

"What do you mean? I'm not going anywhere."

The officer shook her head. "Your house is being treated as a crime scene, and you won't be allowed inside. Besides, it has a lot of smoke and water damage. You'll want to get professionals in to clean."

"But the kidnappers will be calling. Is my phone working?" She wrenched herself free of Jake's grip. "Someone get this thing out of my arm!"

The paramedic, working quickly, removed the I.V. Jake tried to hold her hand, but she couldn't bear to be touched and jerked it away.

"We're checking your phone records now. If the kidnappers deliberately set this fire as a distraction, which seems likely, they'll find some other way to contact you."

Violet knew what she was thinking — if they *wanted* to contact her. Although she'd told Jake she believed they were holding Daisy for ransom, she knew there was another possibility. Babies were often stolen by women who wanted to keep them. Some desperate, childless woman might have seen her picture and decided she needed Daisy to fill her empty arms.

"Jake? Did you see her crib? Was anything else . . . missing from it?"

"It was empty. They took her blanket, and the pink teddy bear she always sleeps with." His voice broke. "I'm glad she has those with her, at least."

Violet wasn't as comforted. Daisy was too young to have chosen a lovey yet, although they always tucked her in with the soft blanket Seth's wife Jenna had knitted for her. Anyone might have wrapped her in the blanket to make her easier to carry — or to hide her — but taking the teddy bear was a more maternal gesture. For Jake's sake, however, she kept the thought to herself.

She climbed out of the ambulance with Jake right behind her. "How can we leave without her?"

"We don't have any choice." He took her in his arms. "I'll take you to Jamie's, and we'll set up headquarters there. We'll get her back, I promise."

*

Jake gave the police Jamie's address, and they both dictated their various phone numbers. Violet called her parents in Connecticut, asking them to meet her at Jamie's apartment as soon as possible.

Then, because he didn't think she could bear to do it, he went inside the smoky townhouse and packed an overnight bag for her. The policewoman accompanied him. He tried not to take it personally that he'd been told not to leave town, and his every movement was being observed. Of course they would treat him, and even Violet, as suspects; what bothered him was that he *felt* guilty, even if he wasn't sure why. Most likely Violet was right, and the ad campaign had inspired someone to take their baby and hold her for ransom. Which meant it was his fault for not following his instincts and saying no to Violet. He'd never been good at saying no to any woman, but she was especially persuasive. No more, he vowed.

Self-conscious under the woman's watchful eyes, he scooped up underwear, tee-shirts and sweatpants from Violet's drawers and tossed them into the overnight bag he found in her closet. In the bathroom, he added everything from the top of the vanity, and her shampoo and body wash from the shower. Anything he'd missed, she could borrow from him or Jamie, or from the cache of personal items left behind by Jamie's girls. Although he recognized he was performing an intimate service, there was nothing sexual about it. He just wanted to take care of Violet — the way he'd failed to take care of Daisy.

Before he returned to Violet, he made a call to Jamie. He needed to warn him that his apartment was about to become a beehive of activity, and he didn't want to say the words "Daisy is missing" in front of her. To his surprise, Jamie told him their Uncle Matt was there; he'd come into the city to see his doctor and get his cast removed. Although he knew it was illogical, it comforted him to know that Matt, the closest thing he had to a father, would be on the scene. Although there was nothing he, or anyone, could do.

He was glad he'd forewarned his brother, because the block he lived on was already lined with police cruisers and plain black sedans when Jake steered his rental car into the underground parking garage twenty minutes later. He and Violet were forced to show I.D. to one uniformed officer, then escorted on the elevator to the penthouse by another.

When they entered the apartment, Jamie rose from one of the leather living room sofas and took Violet in his arms. A tall man dressed in khakis and a white polo shirt joined them.

"Violet and Jake, this is Ted Forrester, he's the lead FBI agent on the case."

Jake was surprised by the man's casual attire, since agents in the movies were always dressed in dark suits. Ted even had a day's growth of dark stubble. The earpiece he wore to keep in touch with the other investigators was the only thing official-looking about him.

"Forgive the way I'm dressed, Mr. Macintyre," he said as he shook Jake's hand with a reassuringly firm grip. "I was called in from my vacation to handle this case."

"Thank you, Agent Forrester. I want my baby back." Violet's voice started out strong, but broke down with her last words.

Forrester nodded, grim-faced, as he shook her hand. "Then let's get to work, shall we?"

Jamie steered Violet to the sofa where he'd been sitting, and the FBI agent indicated Jake should sit next to him on the one across from it. A second agent was perched on the edge of the sofa, typing on a laptop computer in front of him on the coffee table. Two others stood on the periphery of the room. As he was about to sit, he saw his Uncle Matt, who had risen from his chair and held out his arms to him.

He indicated the crutches propped against the armchair. "I'm real wobbly on these things, so come here and give your old uncle a hug." Jake felt so fragile he was afraid Matt's bear-like embrace and slap on the back might kill him. "We'll get your baby back."

When everyone was seated, Forrester asked Violet and Jake to put their cell phones on the table. "I expect the perpetrator will try to contact one of you. We already have your numbers, and we may be able to get some useful information that way. But forget everything you've ever heard about keeping the caller on the line so we'll have time to trace the call. That isn't necessary. Just listen to what he — or *she* — has to say, write down the directions, and don't say anything that might make him mad. Got it?"

They both nodded, and he continued. "It appears the person who did this started a fire outside your laundry room, Miss Gallagher. While the babysitter, Mrs. Cornelius, was distracted, they went in the front door and took the baby. Then they set a second fire in the area of the foyer, so she couldn't get upstairs and see the baby was gone."

"But . . . how did they get in the front door?" Jake asked. "Was there any sign of forced entry?" Violet's front door was entirely visible from the street, and he knew the fire had been set soon after dark. Would the kidnapper have risked someone seeing him while he spent time working on the lock?

Forrester turned his serious, grey-eyed gaze on him. "The firemen did a lot of damage to the front door. Without checking to see if it was open, they slammed an axe into it. We're sending an expert to examine what remains."

Jake sighed and rubbed his face. His hand came away black. "So you have a nice theory. Do you have any evidence?"

"We did find one piece of evidence at the scene so far, outside the laundry room where the fire was started." He took a clear plastic evidence bag out of his briefcase and laid it on the table.

Jake leaned in close. Inside the bag was a good-sized cigarette butt, bent but not crushed.

"It's a Marlboro Menthol Lite," the FBI agent told them. "Do you know anyone who smokes them?"

Violet shrugged. "I don't know anyone who smokes."

Jake, however, had recently seen someone remove a cigarette from the distinctive green and white pack. The knowledge changed everything, and it changed nothing. At least, he told himself, he'd be able to reassure Violet that she had no culpability in the baby's kidnapping. The blame was all his now.

"Uncle Matt, where's Carrie?"

The big man shook his head. He knew what Jake was implying. "She would never do such a thing. Besides, she quit smoking."

Everyone spoke at once after that, but Violet's voice was the only one Jake heard. "What does Carrie have to do with this? How does Matt know her?"

Ted Forrester raised his hand for silence. "Mr. Macintyre, please start at the beginning."

Violet remained silent while Jake explained how Carrie had gone from being Daisy's nanny to Matt's aide. The first time he dared to look in her direction, she was staring at him in horror, like he was a rat she'd just discovered in Daisy's crib. He couldn't blame her — he'd just remembered Carrie telling him her boyfriend wanted her "to do things for money." The second time he glanced at her, after he told them about Carrie babysitting for Daisy at the townhouse, she had covered her face with her hands.

"Mr. Macintyre — Matt — where do you believe this woman to be at the moment?" the agent asked his uncle when Jake finally stopped talking.

"I *believe* she's at the movies with her sister, which is where she told me she was going when she dropped me off here after my doctor's appointment. She's coming back at eleven and we're driving home to Wickham tonight." He gripped the arms of his chair as he spoke, and Jake knew he would be up and pacing around if it didn't require the use of the crutches he'd just gotten that day.

Forrester flipped open his notebook and began to fire questions at him. "What's her sister's name? Where does she live?"

"I don't know! Listen, is there lipstick on that cigarette butt? Carrie was wearing lipstick today, real bright stuff."

The man shook his head. "There's no visible stain, although the lab analysis will tell us more."

Violet *did* jump up. "Her lipstick could have worn off. It's obvious this woman took Daisy, she's probably been planning it ever since I fired her. Any idiot would have known she should be kept away from Daisy!"

She looked around as though she were wondering why she was standing up or where she might go, then took the few steps to Matt's chair and dropped to her knees in front of him. "Please Matt, I know you don't want to believe she did this. But tell us anything you know that might help find Daisy."

Sighing, he reached forward and touched her face. "There is something I know, and it looks bad for Carrie, I have to admit."

"What is it, sir?" The agent held his pen poised above his notebook.

"About a week ago, I heard her yelling at someone in the kitchen. I thought it was the stupid dog. By the time I got in there in that danged wheelchair I saw she'd been talking on the phone — her hand was still on it. I wanted to ask her about it, but she shook her head. Instead she asked me if I would get my phone number changed. I did it the next morning. Didn't ask any questions, cause I just figured that loser boyfriend of hers had gotten my number somehow."

Jake — the "idiot" who'd brought this fiend into Violet's home — held his splitting head in his hands. The locks at Violet's had been changed after Carrie was fired, but she'd spent several hours alone there since then. There were spare keys hanging on a hook in the kitchen, and it would have been easy for her to snag one or have one made. She could have even put Daisy in her stroller and walked to the hardware store.

"But, don't you see?" Matt continued. "She hung up on the guy, and we had the number changed. *He* may have done it, but I know she didn't help him."

Jake's cell phone rang, breaking the moment of silence that followed Matt's heated proclamation. Ted caught his eye and nodded; he slid a pad of paper and a pencil toward him.

"Macintyre here."

"We have the baby, and we want $500,000 for her safe return."

Chapter Fourteen

Jake was reasonably certain the muffled voice was a man's, but that didn't mean Carrie wasn't his accomplice. He thought about confronting him, asking if he was Joe, but decided it would be safer to stick to the guidelines the FBI agent had given him.

"How do we know she's okay?"

Violet gasped, then covered her mouth. He was momentarily distracted by the panic in her eyes — the same panic he was feeling in his gut.

The man laughed, a sound that made the hairs on the back of Jake's neck stand up. "Well, I could make her cry, but you don't want that, do you? She's sleeping with her pink teddy bear, safe and sound."

"The money. When and where?" Jake picked up the pencil.

"Leave it at midnight in Copp's Hill Cemetery, and come alone. No cops, or you'll never see your little flower again."

Jake wrote down the amount, but laughed when he realized the foolishness of the kidnappers instructions. "Midnight? I don't know what world you're living in, you scumbag, but in mine the banks aren't open."

The muffled voice swore, then became totally inaudible as he spoke to someone away from the phone. "Ten o'clock tomorrow morning," he said to Jake a moment later. "Get the money in hundred dollar bills, put it in a backpack and leave it next to Cotton Mather's tombstone. Walk away. An hour later you'll get a call telling you where to pick up your kid."

"Ten a.m.," Jake repeated for the benefit of the others in the room. "If you hurt her, I'll . . ." The line had gone dead. He threw the phone on the table so hard it skidded all the way across.

Jamie caught it and set it down gently, then put his arm around Violet, who was sobbing soundlessly. "The guy is so stupid he didn't know you can't get cash tonight?"

"First of all, was it a man's voice?" Ted asked Jake.

"Yes. It sounded like he had something over his mouth or the phone, maybe a piece of cloth."

The agent tapped his pencil against his notebook. "He called your phone, not Miss Gallagher's. Any idea why?"

Jake had to swallow hard to get the answer past the lump in his throat. "Carrie knew my cell phone number." He raised his eyes to Violet. "I'm so sorry."

*

Violet ignored Jake. His pathetic apology would do nothing to bring back her baby. *Her* baby. What he'd done filled her with a fury so intense it was frightening, but she was angry at herself as well. Her instincts had told her to keep Jake out of her life — and Daisy's — but the first moment she'd found him useful, she'd let him in. Inch by inch, she'd let him, until he'd taken over. He thought he knew what was best for Daisy — he thought he knew best about *everything* — and he'd acted without consulting her. Even with proof Carrie had neglected Daisy, and worse, he'd brought her back into her life. It was, in a word, unforgivable. If — *when* — she got Daisy back, she would do everything in her power to make sure Jake would be out of her life forever.

She shot him a look she hoped was so scathing contact with her would become his new biggest phobia. To avoid it, he'd willingly walk through any fire.

"I'll get the money," she told the FBI agent. "I phoned my parents on my way over here, and they chartered a plane to fly up from Connecticut. I don't have that much cash available, but my stepfather will provide the rest."

"Violet, I want to help . . ."

She ignored Jake. "Just so we're clear, Agent Forrester, Mr. Macintyre has no legal rights here."

Jake opened his mouth to speak, then apparently changed his mind. His face crumpled, but she had no sympathy for him.

The second agent showed Ted something on the computer screen, then he spoke to Violet. "There's a chance we'll have your baby back before you have to pay the ransom. We already know the call was made from a walk-up pay phone in the North End, in the same area as Copp's Hill Cemetery. Now I need you to tell me everything you know about the former nanny."

"Carrie didn't do this," Matt said, hoisting himself up and hobbling out of the room on his crutches. "You'll see."

Violet ignored him. "Her name is Carrie Benedict. I hired her through The Cabot Agency, I'm sure they have much more information than I have. Elizabeth Cabot is the owner."

"We'll track down her last known address in Boston and send someone to speak to anyone they find there." He raised a finger to let Violet know he was listening to someone on his earpiece.

At the same time, they heard the ding of the elevator arriving in the foyer. Violet looked at her watch. It was eleven-fifteen. If everything had gone smoothly, her mother and David could have made it to Boston by now.

"That must be my mother." She jumped up to greet her; she'd never needed her more than she did at that moment.

Tears were sliding down her face and she was ready to throw herself into her mother's arms when the elevator door slid open. But there were only two people inside, and neither of them was her mother. The same uniformed policeman who had escorted her and Jake when they arrived had a firm grip on the second person, whose hands were cuffed behind her back. Carrie.

*

"He didn't ask me to kidnap Daisy, and I had no idea he was going to do it." Carrie, pale and trembling in spite of Matt's big arm around her, had just told the investigators that Joe's brother, a small-time hood with a police record, lived in the North End. They were sending officers to the address she gave them even as she told her story.

"He said he'd seen Miss Gallagher and her baby in the ads, and that she had a lot of money. That I'd blown it for him by getting fired, but he had a plan for how I could make it up to him."

"What did you say?" Forrester asked her.

"I hung up. I told him I wasn't afraid of him anymore, and he'd better stay away from me."

"But how did he know to call you at Matt's?" Violet asked her.

Carrie turned her tear-stained face in her direction for the first time, and Violet saw how much the former nanny had changed. It wasn't just the make-up and the flattering hairstyle, either. Despite the woman's current anxiety, she seemed more self-possessed, and her gaze met and held Violet's across the coffee table.

"He said his sister-in-law — her name is Angel — saw the interview you did with Jake. She told him Jake was born and raised in Wickham, and Joe had a hunch and started calling every Macintyre in Wickham. When he got to Matt's number, of course I answered."

"Got to get Caller ID," Matt muttered to himself.

"Miss Gallagher, I would never have hurt you or your baby, but I'm so sorry now I didn't tell anyone what Joe said about you. He's a real bad guy, I know that, but I never imagined . . ."

"It's hard to believe this of anyone, but it happens," Jake said from behind Violet. "He's not just bad, he's stupid and cruel. That's the worst combination there is." She'd sensed him standing behind her, listening to Carrie's explanation, and she knew he was talking about his own stepfather as well as Joe.

"Angel — well, she's a mom. A good one. I know she'll keep Daisy safe."

Violet thought about the pink teddy bear and Daisy's blanket, and wanted desperately to believe Carrie was right. Although she was more optimistic than she'd been earlier, Daisy wasn't back in her arms yet. There was no relief for her just because the woman had shown up when she said she would, even if it did mean she probably had no part in the kidnapping.

Jake's instincts about the former nanny might have been accurate, but he shouldn't have gone behind her back or withheld the crucial information that a woman she'd fired had been left to care for her baby, alone. How could she ever trust him again?

When the elevator dinged again, she rushed to the foyer. This time it was her parents, but her heart fell because it wasn't a policewoman holding her baby. "Violet, it's too soon," Jake whispered to her, even though he'd rushed to meet the elevator for the same reason she had. "We'll hear something in a few minutes."

Then her mother's arms were around her and she was enveloped in the subtle scent of Sandra's signature perfume. David Gallagher was introducing himself to the FBI agent and everyone else in the room, and demanding an update. "Where is my granddaughter? What's being done to find her?"

"Everyone be quiet!" Forrester raised his hand to the room like a cop directing traffic. Then he did something amazing — he smiled. "They have the baby, and she's fine. She'll be here in fifteen minutes."

It was the longest fifteen minutes of Violet's life. In fact, it was seventeen, but then the elevator arrived and a beaming policewoman handed Daisy to her mother. The baby smiled and nuzzled against Violet, but as soon as everyone else crowded around them, talking in loud, excited voices, she began to wail.

"We need to give Violet and Daisy some space," her mother said. Everyone went back to the living room, while Violet stayed in the foyer, talking to Daisy and soothing her. At the same time she examined her from head to toe. She appeared to be unharmed, as Forrester had said.

After several minutes, she finally took her eyes off her precious baby. Ignoring all the happy faces in the living room, her gaze locked on the one face that wasn't. Jake stood on the far side of the room, watching Violet and Daisy. His lips turned up in a sad smile and tears glinted in the corners of his eyes when their eyes met.

"Let's go see your daddy," she whispered to Daisy.

When he saw his family headed toward him, Jake's smile morphed into the real thing. He held his arms out to Daisy and her body strained toward him while they were still several feet away. Violet remembered when the baby reaching out to Jake would have made her jealous and protective. No more. Daisy didn't need protection from her father.

She transferred the baby to his arms. "I'm so sorry," she said in a voice so low only he could hear it.

Daisy squealed as her father planted kisses on her chubby neck. "She doesn't smell right," he said to Violet. "We need to give her a bath."

She nodded. She'd noticed the same thing. Daisy smelled foreign, and it was an unpleasant reminder she'd been out of their care for far too long.

"Wait. Did you say you were *sorry*? What do *you* have to be sorry for?"

"I didn't listen when you said the exposure of the ad campaign could be bad for Daisy. Her kidnapping was all my fault." Violet knew now her mistake hadn't been letting Jake into their lives, it had been not trusting him enough. Not that she wanted to turn the decision-making over to him — he shouldn't have let Carrie into her townhouse without talking to her first — but maybe they could learn to communicate better. They were Daisy's parents. They'd have to work together from now on, whether they were in the same room or on different continents.

Jake shook his head. He shifted Daisy to his left arm and

embraced Violet with his right, pulling the three of them into a tight circle. "I could have said no. I decided I was overreacting, seeing danger where there wasn't any. There's always risk, but you have to live your life. It will be hard for us not to be overprotective of Daisy now. Hard for *you*."

"No, you were right the first time. It will be hard for *us*."

He pulled back and gave her a questioning look, but Daisy was squirming and rubbing her eyes. She took her from Jake. "This baby needs a bath and a bottle. Do I have a volunteer to run to the store for diapers and formula?"

*

When Violet woke the next morning, the terror of the previous day came rushing back in her first moments of consciousness, and she bolted upright to find herself in an unfamiliar room.

"Relax, everything's fine." It was Jake's voice, and Jake's comforting hand on her arm. She remembered then that she was in the guest room in Jamie's luxurious penthouse.

She sat up and turned to face Jake. He was stretched across Daisy, who was nestled between them with a pillow on either side of her, still asleep despite the disturbance Violet had created. Since a king-sized bed in the center of the guest room was their only sleeping option in Jamie's apartment, and it was too heavy to move against a wall, they'd been forced to share the bed. Jake had assured her co-sleeping was a common practice in many parts of the world and neither of them would roll over and crush the baby. She'd pretended to believe him, but had added the pillows and planned to stay awake all night, just in case.

"I can't believe I slept. Did Daisy wake up at all?"

He shook his head. "I think she's officially sleeping through the night."

"That's not the only 'first.' This is the third time I've gone to sleep in the same bed with you, but the first time you were still in it when I woke up in the morning."

His laugh made Daisy startle, and she looked around in confusion for a moment, then settled her gaze on Violet. She smiled and wriggled her whole body in excitement.

"I couldn't desert my post. Daisy might have climbed over the pillows, rolled over four or five times, and fallen off the bed."

The baby turned her head toward Jake and laughed.

"See, even Daisy thinks it's funny."

Violet was relieved the baby was in such good spirits. "Do you think she'll remember what happened on some level?" Was her child going to be traumatized, prone for the rest of her life to fears and phobias? If only she'd listened to Jake when he urged her not to do the ad campaign.

He sat up and lifted Daisy to his bare shoulder, where she was content, for the moment, to rest her head. Violet would have liked to do the same. "I think she'll be fine. We just have to make her feel as loved and secure as possible."

Violet sighed. "*We*, Jake? I know you're Daisy's father and I want you to be as involved in her life as you can or want to be, but won't it be hard for you to make her feel 'loved and secure' from Zimbabwe?"

"Zimbabwe? I thought I was going to Peru."

His flip response brought tears to her eyes, and she had to turn her head away so he wouldn't see. As she'd fought sleep the night before, she'd thought about everything that had happened, and decided she needed to keep Jake in Daisy's life. In *hers*, too. Together they'd have a better chance of making good parenting decisions. If it meant he was only physically present for brief periods, then she'd do her best to remind Daisy of him the rest of the time. In a world where you could spy on your nanny, that should be easy, right? He could take a laptop with a camera everywhere he went.

This morning, however, with Jake so close she could feel the heat from his body, it didn't seem like a very good plan.

Violet felt the bedsprings move as he slid over beside her. Daisy flung herself at her mother, and after shifting the baby into her lap, Jake slid his arm around her and pulled them both close to him. She shivered at the contact with his bare chest. When they went to bed last night, the joke had been that Jamie had no pajamas to lend his brother, and after asking her permission, he'd climbed into bed wearing only a fresh pair of white boxers.

Jake touched her face, turned it toward him and kissed her lips while Daisy pummeled them both, trying to get some attention. "Violet, I'm not going to Peru."

Did he mean he was staying in Boston, or going somewhere else? She held her breath until he completed the thought.

"How can I leave Daisy? How can I leave *you*? I love you both. No more running away for me."

"But Jake, will loving us be enough?" Monty had loved her mother. He'd most likely loved her and Seth, too. But it hadn't been enough to make him stay. She didn't want to have Jake in her life now, only to lose him later.

"Violet, do you love me?"

The last time she'd told him she did, he'd moved out the next day. What was the right answer? She took a deep breath. In her profession, and her life, the only right answer was the honest one. "Yes, Jake, I love you."

"Ga!" cried Daisy, and pounded Jake on the nose. He broke eye contact with Violet and grabbed Daisy's fist.

"Is this the kind of treatment I can expect from my new family?" he asked the baby.

The word brought a mist of tears to Violet's eyes, but she was still not certain they were doing the right thing. Or even what it *was* they were doing. "Jake, you love to travel. You *need* to travel for your work . . ."

"And I will, but only for shorter periods. Or you and Daisy will come with me. You're a journalist. Haven't you ever wanted to get the stories outside your own backyard?"

She smiled. Suddenly the world was full of possibilities. All she'd had to do was stop making plans and let life happen. Let *Jake* happen. "I'd consider it."

"There's plenty of time to discuss the details. But first, I have an important question to ask you."

Violet's heart thumped in her chest. "Go ahead."

His amber eyes gazed directly into hers. "Violet Gallagher, will you . . ." Daisy, who had been whining softly, chose that moment to erupt into an angry, shrieking cry. "Will you . . . get our daughter a bottle? And a dry diaper?"

She rubbed the slight growth of reddish beard on his chin, shivering at the thought of all that was to come. "Yes, my love. I will."

Epilogue

Violet's heart thudded as she watched Richard Rayburn open the envelope with the name of the winner of the Thompson Award for News Excellence inside. The word in the industry was that she had no serious competition, but you never knew how these things would go. Jake gripped her hand under the tablecloth and she smiled at him. She'd told him she had to be prepared to clap her hands raw and appear genuinely happy if one of her rivals won, which would be harder than producing her story had been.

Richard grinned and his gaze zeroed in on her from the stage. "Violet Gallagher, for her story 'Abuse, America's Dirty Little Secret.'"

Jake helped her up from her chair, and kissed her full on the lips. "Was there ever any doubt?" he whispered in her ear. "Be careful in those shoes," he added.

Violet laughed and shook her head. "Stop worrying so much." Even so, she stepped gingerly around the tables and chairs as the crowd applauded, and when she reached the steps to the stage she realized Jake was right about the stylish high heels she'd insisted on wearing. There was no handrail, and she couldn't see her feet. Would she *ever* learn to listen to his advice? Noticing her hesitation, Richard rushed down and gave her his arm.

"Congratulations, Mrs. Macintyre," he said as he escorted her up to the dais. "It looks like you've hit the jackpot."

As she waited for the applause to end, her eyes scanned the room. The first person she saw, as always, was Jake. If the glow of his tan and his golden curls didn't draw her attention, the fact that he was clapping hard and whistling would have. Had it been three years since she'd first picked him out of a crowd, at a time when she was feeling sorry for herself because she had no special someone to celebrate her success with her? Could so much have changed in such a short time?

She smiled at each of the special people standing at the table with Jake. Matt, Jamie, and Seth — it was like having three brothers to tease and torment her now instead of just one. David Gallagher, who was so pleased that she still used his name professionally after her marriage, with her mother at his side, tears on her face but her make-up, of course, intact.

The only loved one missing was Daisy, who wasn't invited to this grown-up event and had to spend the evening with a babysitter. But Daisy's little sister was here, she thought, feeling a foot wiggle inside of her. Placing her hand on the mound of her belly, she noticed with surprise that a space had opened up above it — her baby had dropped into the birth canal sometime this evening. It was time for her to speak, but her only thought was a fervent wish that her water not break in front of all these people.

Locking eyes with Jake got her back on track. "Two years ago, I met a woman who was being abused." She wished Carrie could be here tonight, and knew Matt did too. "I didn't understand why it took her so long to do something about it. After getting to know her, I wanted to understand. So I did this story."

She'd done it not just for Carrie, but for Amanda, the mother-in-law she would never know. Donations to the local battered women's shelter had increased dramatically after the story ran, as had discussions in the newspapers and on the Internet. That was far more satisfying to her than any award; the recognition by her peers was just a sweet bonus.

Although she'd planned to say more, a wave of pressure low in her groin made her catch her breath. She forced a smile and simply said, "Thank you for this wonderful award, it means the world to me."

Jake ran onto the stage as applause filled the ballroom. "Violet?

Is something happening?" He guided her back down to the table, where their family waited.

"Yes, I think it is. But don't worry, there's plenty of time to go back for my overnight bag, and to say goodbye to Daisy."

"Say goodbye to Daisy?" Her mother had overheard her and her face lit up with excitement. "You're in labor! I'm finally going to find out the sex of this grandchild. You know, if it's another girl, Rose would be a lovely name. Or have I already suggested that?"

Violet and Jake looked at each other and laughed. They had wanted the sex of the baby to be a surprise, but an unwitting nurse had spilled the ultrasound results at her last checkup. Although they hadn't told anyone else yet, they *had* picked out a name. Amanda Rose, after Jake's mother. Sandra would have to be content with that.

Another contraction squeezed Violet's insides, mild but still strong enough to show on her face. Jake collected her evening bag and took her elbow.

"We need to hurry. Your bag, my camera, and the birthing plan are all at home."

She laughed. "Which means things are already not going the way we planned. Jake, when are you going to learn to lighten up and be more spontaneous? You know what they say about the best laid plans . . ."

About the Author

Although she was admonished to "stop making things up" when she was a child, Elizabeth Palmer never did. She took early retirement from her job in IT, and now spends her days with the ever-changing cast of characters in her head, her handsome husband, and the requisite author's cat.

In the mood for more Crimson Romance? Check out *Looking for Prince Charming* at CrimsonRomance.com.

Printed in Dunstable, United Kingdom